W9-BIO-309

"You wrote me we didn't have a marriage at all."

Nicky's nails were digging into her palms. "I suppose it was more like an...arrangement."

The silence was deafening. "I see," Blake said at last, his voice ominously low.

"A convenient arrangement for you," she heard herself say. "You'd go on your trips, and whenever you came home I was conveniently there for you, to cook your meals and be available in bed."

"I don't think," he said at last, "that this is a fruitful discussion." His voice was cold with barely restrained fury. "I have no desire to have an argument over something that's been dead and gone for over four years."

Ever since **KAREN VAN DER ZEE** was a child growing up in Holland, she wanted to do two things: write books and travel. She's been very lucky. Her American husband's work as a development economist has taken them to many exotic locations. They were married in Kenya, had their first daughter in Ghana and their second in the United States. They spent two fascinating years in Indonesia. Since then they've added a son to the family. They live in Virginia, but not permanently!

Books by Karen van der Zee

HARLEQUIN PRESENTS
1350—JAVA NIGHTS
1422—KEPT WOMAN
1486—THE IMPERFECT BRIDE
1686—PASSIONATE ADVENTURE
1729—MAKING MAGIC

KAREN VAN DER ZEE

An Inconvenient Husband

Harlequin Books

TORONTO • NEW YORK • LONDON
AMSTERDAM • PARIS • SYDNEY • HAMBURG
STOCKHOLM • ATHENS • TOKYO • MILAN
MADRID • WARSAW • BUDAPEST • AUCKLAND

ISBN 0-373-11886-4

AN INCONVENIENT HUSBAND

First North American Publication 1997.

Copyright © 1996 by Karen van der Zee.

This edition published by arrangement with Harlequin Books S.A.

Printed in U.S.A.

PROLOGUE

NICKY'S hand trembled as she reached for the phone on her father's desk, pushing aside the tiny cup of thick black coffee the servant had brought her a few moments ago. She had all the jitters she needed without the caffeine.

She dialed the number and heard the ringing of the phone on the other side of the world. Her heart was beating so frantically, it was frightening. She stared out the window as the phone kept ringing, at the view of palm trees and the tall minaret of the mosque silhouetted against the cobalt blue Moroccan sky.

Finally the ringing stopped and a female hotel employee answered the phone in English, her voice accented and cheerful. The line was clear, as if the voice came from the house next door rather than from Manilla in the Philippines.

Nicky closed her eyes and braced herself, her chest heavy with anxiety. "I'd like to speak to Mr. Blake Chandler, please. I don't know the room number."

"One moment, please."

The phone rang again. In Blake's room. Finally, his voice—short, clipped, deep. The voice she loved more than any other in the world. The voice of her husband.

Yet her heart was not racing with love and excitement. It was thundering with trepidation.

"Blake, it's Nicky," she said.

"Nicky?" He sounded surprised. "I'm glad you're calling. I was about to call you. How are you?"

She swallowed. "I'm fine."

I'm not fine, she corrected silently. *I'm scared. Blake, I'm so scared.*

"And your mother?"

"She's doing much better."

Nicky was in Morocco with her parents because her mother had become ill and she'd wanted to be with her. Her father worked for the U.S. Agency for International Development and he and her mother had lived in Marrakech for the past year.

Nicky tried to relax her hand gripping the receiver. "Why were you going to call me?" she asked. *Please tell me you miss me. Please tell me you love me and can't wait to be home together again.*

"There's a problem with the project," Blake said instead. "It will take a couple of days to straighten out. I'll be home two days late, on Saturday, same flight schedule."

Disappointment tasted bitter in her mouth. He wasn't telling her what she needed to hear. She swallowed. "It's all right. As it turns out, I've changed my plans, as well." She tried to sound matter-of-fact. "I'm going to see Sophie in Rome on my way back to the States. She's having her baby and I...I think it's nice for me to be there."

"How long will you stay?" A businesslike question. His voice was expressionless.

She swallowed hard. *Go ahead, do it*, urged the little voice inside her.

Next week Blake would come home and the plan had been for her to be back in Washington, as well. She closed her eyes, steeling herself. "Three weeks," she said, feeling her heart grow cold.

A slight pause. "We won't see each other, then," came his voice. "You won't be back home until after I leave again for Guatemala."

Her hands shook. She clenched her left one hard around the receiver. "Right." She gulped in air. "Do you mind?"

They had not seen each other in almost three months and if she didn't go straight home next week they wouldn't see each other for another month or so until Blake came back from his next consulting trip to Guatemala. And she was asking him if he minded.

"You have to be there for your friends," Blake stated. There was no inflection in his voice. "I'll manage. I'm a big boy."

She felt as if she were suffocating. He doesn't care! came the desperate thought. He didn't care last time and he doesn't care now. What was it he had said last time? *If your mother needs you, then of course you have to stay*. That had been five weeks ago when she had called him and told him she wouldn't be home when he came back from his business trip because her mother still wasn't very well.

Which had been true enough, but the virus she'd caught had not been serious, just took its own sweet time to run its course, making her mother tired and cranky.

Nicky could have gone home to Washington and spent time with her husband while he was back in the country preparing for his next consulting job overseas. She could have been home cooking food for him, sleeping in his arms, making love, planning the future.

Instead she'd decided to stay at her parents' house in Morocco and Blake had not objected. He had not said he minded, that he would miss her, that the house was lonely without her.

Now, after not having seen her for three months, he still didn't say any of those things. He told her he could manage without her while she was in Rome to see her friend Sophie.

Of course he would manage. He'd managed without her for years and years. He was an independent, self-sufficient man with a career that took him all over the world. She had known that when she had married him eighteen months ago. It had not bothered her—her father's job had taken her quite a few places, too, when she was a child. She understood her husband's life-style, his work.

They'd married and made plans for the future. As soon as she had her journalism degree, she planned to go with him on his trips, write her articles about travel and food, maybe even a book. They'd be together most of the time. So many plans, so much to look forward to.

And now, her degree in her pocket, her dreams were crumbling like stale cake, dry and tasteless. Blake could do without her.

He doesn't need me, she thought, tears hot behind her eyes. I'm convenient and comfortable, but I'm not essential to him. She saw him in her mind's eye, the tall, confident man with calm gray eyes and uncompromising, square chin. The man whose strong arms fitted so perfectly around her, whose body made magic with hers. A heavy weight settled on her chest and she sucked in a painful breath. There hadn't been magic for a long time.

"How's the food over there?" she asked, and she could hear the odd wobble in her voice.

"I've got you some recipes—you'll find them interesting." She loved food and cooking, all kinds, simple and exotic. She loved looking at displays of fruit, spices, vegetables, loved the colors and shapes and fragrances. Her husband the world traveler brought her gifts of cookbooks and recipes from faraway places for her collection.

"Thank you." Again the wobble in her voice.

"Nicky? Are you all right? You sound strange."

"I'm fine," she lied. "The air is so dusty here, it makes my throat feel scratchy." This was not a lie, but the fact was irrelevant.

They talked for a while. About his work, about the magazine article she was writing about Moroccan food, about how lucky they were to be missing the bad weather at home in Washington, D.C.

Later that night she lay in bed, her stomach churning with anxiety, praying she would just sink away into oblivion and not dream the dream that kept coming back time after time. A dream that made her cry when she awakened.

Here she was, in her parents' home in one of the most exotic places on earth, a place of deserts and camels and Berber nomads, a place of veiled women, busy souks and ancient mosques, yet where she really wanted to be was in her own small town house in Washington, D.C., which at this very moment was battling the leftovers of a tropical storm. She wanted to be in her own bed in the arms of the man she loved. She wanted him to tell her he loved her, that he had missed her terribly. That those long absences were harder and harder to bear. That from now on he wanted her with him on his trips.

She knew it wasn't going to happen.

She knew she was losing him.

CHAPTER ONE

IT WAS a wonderful party. Nicky sipped her wine, knowing she should be enjoying herself rather than letting the odd sense of foreboding spoil her fun. She surveyed the interesting mix of people. Women flaunted bright sarongs and silk saris, as well as fashionable designer dresses. Men sported well-cut suits or trousers and silk *batek* shirts. From the large, elegant sitting room with its beautiful Chinese furniture, the festivities spilled out into the jasmine-scented garden bathing in the tropical Malaysian night air.

It was a wonderful party.

And something was very wrong.

Nicky clenched her fingers around the stem of her crystal glass and glanced over at her father, a tall and distinguished man who stood out a head taller than most people at the party. He looked worried and she didn't like it. She'd arrived in Kuala Lumpur two weeks ago for an extended visit and working vacation, and she'd sensed immediately that not all was well with her father. It had something to do with business, Nicky knew, something involving an unscrupulous Hong Kong investment company causing problems, but he'd told her it wasn't serious.

She didn't believe it for a minute.

Nazirah appeared by her side in a rustle of emerald silk. "Did you see that great-looking guy come in a minute ago?" she whispered.

Nicky shrugged indifferently. "Which one?"

Nazirah rolled her eyes. "Come with me. I'm going to fix my face."

In the lavishly appointed bathroom, they stood next to each other in front of the mirror. They were the same height, five feet two, equally slim, but that's where the resemblance stopped. Nazirah was half American, half Malaysian, with very long, sleek, black hair and blue eyes, while Nicky had very short, curly auburn hair and brown eyes.

Nazirah took a tube of lipstick out of her small clutch bag and unscrewed the top. "Are you sure you didn't see him?" she asked, glancing over at Nicky. "The really tall one with the great shoulders? Dark hair, gray eyes. Calm and composed looking, but you just know there's all that passion brewing underneath. He—"

"No," said Nicky curtly, and fished in her bag for lipstick, as well.

"Oh, right, you're not interested in men." Nazirah eyed her curiously in the mirror.

And certainly not in tall handsome ones with great shoulders and gray eyes, Nicky added silently. She felt a stab of pain. Four years after the divorce and still she had those sudden moments of anguish set off by a word, a memory, the scent of roses. She put the lipstick back in her bag. "What time do you want to get started tomorrow?" she asked, to change the subject. Nazirah was going to take her to explore the Central Market.

Nazirah's parents were friends of Nicky's father, and she'd offered to be Nicky's guide and translator on her ventures through Kuala Lumpur. Nicky was doing research on a magazine article about street food, which involved roaming the markets and streets sampling snacks from the ubiquitous vendors.

"The earlier, the better," stated Nazirah. "I'll pick you up at seven. You know, I just love your dress. Classy, but sexy. Where did you buy it? Washington?"

Nicky nodded. She loved the dress herself. Made of a soft silk crepe in various shades of aquamarine, it was long and slim-fitting and made her appear less short. High heels, of course, and long earrings, helped. "Let's get a drink. I'm thirsty."

The bar was set out in the garden where semi-hidden garden lamps discreetly augmented the moonlight, creating a romantic ambience.

"There he is!" whispered Nazirah, squeezing Nicky's arm. "Isn't he something?"

Nicky looked up and froze. Her breath caught in her throat and her heart stopped beating for an instant.

The man was something all right.

Tall and lean in an immaculate tropical suit, he looked the perfect male specimen—fit, healthy and confident. Steely gray eyes were bright in the tanned, angular face, the strong chin indicating purpose and command. Here was a man who was comfortable in the world, comfortable with himself, a man in his prime. A man with an undeniable magnetism.

The man who'd once been her husband.

"Hello, Nicky," said the familiar voice—the voice that made her legs feel weak and her body flush with warmth, even now after all these years.

"Blake?" Nicky whispered. There seemed to be no air to breathe. She was not prepared for this. She felt dizzy with the shock, or the resulting lack of oxygen.

He nodded, his cool gray eyes intent on her face. He extended his hand and automatically she held out hers.

"How are you?" he asked, taking her hand in his. His voice sounded perfectly calm, as if greeting a colleague or acquaintance.

She swallowed at the dryness in her throat. "I'm fine," she managed. His hand was warm and firm and the contact set off a tingling all through her, causing every cell to spring to life with remembered love.

This is crazy, she thought. Crazy, crazy. Here she was, politely shaking hands with a man with whom she'd once shared a bed, whose body she knew intimately. She suppressed a hysterical little laugh and forced herself to smile politely.

"What a surprise to see you here," she said. The understatement of the year. No mere surprise could cause such a tumultuous reaction in her mind and body. No, she wasn't surprised. She was stunned.

He released her hand, but his eyes did not leave her face. "It's a small world."

Well, it was, of course. The expatriate communities in foreign countries were comparatively small. She nodded, not knowing what to say.

"It was good to run into your father again," he said. "Hadn't seen him for years. He told me he'd left USAID and joined the world of private business—a venture capital firm, no less."

"Yes," she said, hearing more the deep timbre of his voice than the words. She couldn't take her eyes off him, as if she were hypnotized, or in some sort of trance.

He took a drink from his glass. "They're involved in some interesting investment projects in China, I understand."

"Yes. All over South East Asia, really. He's just interested in China now that it's opening up." She spoke automatically, not even knowing if she was making sense, not caring. All she saw was the familiar face of the man she had once loved.

Blake looked the same, only a little older. And a little harder, a little rougher around the edges. There were a few strands of gray hair at his temples and his jaw had a steely set. He was thirty-seven now, she realized, ten years older than she. He still emanated the same dynamic vibrations, and he seemed to her more attractive than ever.

"Are you working in Malaysia?" she asked, remembering he'd always loved the Far East, ever since he'd spent two years in Malaysia as a Peace Corps volunteer in his early twenties, before she'd known him. The question came automatically, as if some part of her was going through the motions of making polite conversation while the rest of her was struggling with emotional chaos.

He nodded. "I'm doing research for the World Bank. Tropical fruit."

"What about tropical fruit?"

"Production, processing, exporting—how to develop the business in Malaysia. I spent the last few weeks looking at farms and factories. There's a growing demand for exotic fruit all over the western world."

She nodded. "People want a change from apples and pears. Here come the guavas and the mangos and the soursops."

"I knew you'd understand," he said dryly. He took another swallow from his Scotch. "You're in Malaysia to visit your father?" His tone was polite. He might have been speaking to a total stranger. Something was different about his voice. It was rougher—the voice of someone who'd seen much and expected nothing.

She moistened her lips. "Yes. It's a fascinating place and I thought I'd come for a while and do some writing. With my father living here it was a wonderful opportunity."

He studied her with what seemed detached interest. "You haven't changed."

"Should I have? Did you expect me to?" Her heart was beating erratically. She wished it would calm down.

He shrugged. "I somehow just thought you would have."

"Why?"

Something flickered briefly in his eyes. "I never could imagine you to still be the same person I once knew." He shrugged. "But then, I can't really judge, can I? I don't know you now. I'm just looking at the externals." He gave a polite little smile, but it did not reach his eyes. "And they're as pleasant as they always were."

Always the gentleman. "Thank you," she said, wishing she had a drink. "And as for the rest of me, I imagine I'm pretty much the same person I always was, except older and wiser."

"We grow and we learn," he added casually. Nicky wondered if she heard an undertone of mockery. She found the unsmiling gray gaze disconcerting. But then, what could she expect? Surely not warmth or humor.

"You're still consulting, then?" she commented. When she had met him, years ago, he had worked with her father for the U.S. Agency for International Development, but soon after he'd become an independent consultant working internationally in the field of agricultural economics, often contracting with the World Bank.

He nodded. "That's what I do. I took a two-year teaching position at Cornell a few years ago, for a change of pace, but then decided to go back to consulting. I enjoy doing better than teaching. And how's your career been coming along?"

How polite the conversation. It seemed unreal, as if it were happening on another plane. "I'm doing well." Her articles sold to magazines and newspapers, and she was writing her second book, a hybrid mix of travelogue and cookbook for the more adventurous readers, generously spiced with humor. She wished she could find some humor in the present situation, but it eluded her.

He glanced at her left hand. "Not married again?"

Her heart contracted painfully. "No." She crossed her arms in front of her chest, knowing it made her look defensive, not knowing what else to do with her hands.

One dark eyebrow arched slightly. "I thought you would have."

"Why?"

He lifted his left shoulder fractionally. "You're rather the marrying type, with all your domestic talents." His voice gave nothing away. Once he had enjoyed her domestic talents. Her cooking, especially. She pushed away the memories.

"And you? Are you married again?" Somehow she managed to sound casual, but an odd terror tightened her chest, and she realized in a flash of insight that she didn't want to hear the answer. That she didn't want to know there was another woman in his life.

He gave a dry laugh. "I think I'll save myself the effort."

The terror vanished and she felt an upsurge of hot anger—unexpected, surprising. Effort? What effort had he ever put into their marriage? She clamped down on the feelings. "I wasn't aware being married to me had been such a trial," she commented, trying to sound coolly sophisticated, but knowing she wasn't pulling it off. Her voice shook with emotion.

Because of his career there had been long absences in their short marriage, but when he'd been home between consulting trips, life surely had not been much struggle for him—she'd treated him like a king.

Because she'd loved him. Because she'd thought he was the most wonderful, sexy man she'd ever known. Because she'd been a romantic idiot.

He gave an indifferent shrug. "Let's not go into this, shall we? It hardly matters now." He tossed back the last of his drink.

As if a failed marriage were a mere triviality.

"You never did care, did you?" she said bitterly, feeling her body tense further with remembered pain.

His eyes glittered like cold crystal. "You never bothered to ask. How would you possibly know whether I cared or not?"

"As your wife, I had no trouble telling. I'm glad I got out when I did." She clenched her hands, sorry she'd let the anger escape.

His body stiffened. He shoved his free hand into his pocket and she noticed it was balled into a fist. Anger burned in his eyes.

"You weren't interested in having a discussion when you ended our marriage," he said harshly. "Whether I cared or not was apparently irrelevant to you. Is there any point in having this discussion now, four years later?"

"No, there isn't, you're right," she said frigidly. She whirled around and walked off, knowing she couldn't stand being with him a moment longer, feeling terrified by the sudden onslaught of emotions she'd thought had been buried long ago—anger, bitterness, and a deep, searing anguish.

She had a throbbing headache and her eyes burned treacherously. She'd had enough. All she wanted was to go home and go to bed, fall asleep and forget she'd seen Blake.

Her father's driver took her back to the house, which wasn't too far away. The watchman came running to the gates and opened them to let the car through. She said good-night to the driver and he drove off again to go back to the party to wait for her father.

A small light was on in the entryway, but the rest of the house lay in darkness. The servants had gone home and the place seemed empty and deserted. An odd chill shivered down her back. The place was too big; she wasn't used to all that empty space. Her own apartment in Washington was small and cozy. She'd moved into it after the divorce, not wanting to stay on in the historic Georgetown town house she and Blake had shared during their marriage. She'd wanted a new beginning with nothing to remind her of Blake. Such a silly illusion— as if it were possible to erase Blake from her life. A man like Blake Chandler tended to leave an indelible impression, marking you for life.

The moonlight shining through the palm trees outside threw moving shadows across the furniture and rugs. Beautiful carved teak furniture, exquisite Chinese rugs, silk draperies, ornate brass lamps. The house had been decorated professionally and lacked a personal touch. She knew what her mother would have thought of it: too opulent, too pretentious. Poor Daddy, she thought, you must miss her so. Her mother had died unexpectedly a year ago and her father had been at a loss ever since. He'd taken on a new job, moved to new, exotic surroundings, but it only seemed to accentuate his loneliness.

She turned on a couple of lamps as she found her way to her room which lay at the back of the house. Inside, she switched on the light. She dropped her bag onto a chair, noticing the French doors that opened into the garden were standing slightly ajar.

She had closed them before she left. Hadn't she? She shrugged. Well, maybe not. She bit her lip, feeling uneasy. Something felt…wrong. Some ghostly awareness feathered across her skin, as if something unseen was right here with her—a presence, an energy in the air. She surveyed the room. There was nothing unusual. Everything was just the way she had left it.

She went into the adjoining bathroom, found some aspirin and swallowed it with a glass of water, making a face at herself in the mirror. "You are a nut case," she said out loud.

There were no ghosts in her room; they were in her mind. She felt haunted by shadows from the past, that's what it was. She'd been thrown off her equilibrium because she'd seen Blake again.

"You haven't seen him in four years," she told her reflection. "You're divorced. So what's the big deal?"

She took off her clothes and got ready for bed. She drifted off into a restless sleep, full of images of Blake— Blake sitting by a fire and reading a book. Blake pouring wine, giving her a secret smile. Blake sprawled on the bed, naked, asleep. She wanted to touch him, run her hand over his body, feel his warmth, his strength. She reached out, but her hand did not make contact, no matter how hard she tried, as if some force field protected him from her touch. She awoke, crying.

It took a long time to get back to sleep.

The next morning she was dragged into consciousness by the call to prayer broadcast from the mosque's minaret. It was almost six, and the faint glimmer of dawn filtered through the thin curtains. She listened to the monotonous chanting, knowing the meaning, but not understanding the Arabic words.

She lay still in bed, until the sun washed the room in the bright light of a new day.

"You just disappeared," Nazirah accused her an hour later as they were on their way to the Central Market in town. The chauffeur-driven car was compliments of Nazirah's father.

"I had a headache."

"I saw you talking to that guy. Did he tell you who he is?"

"A consultant on a World Bank contract. He's here only temporarily." Nicky tried to sound bored. She did not want to discuss Blake. She did not even want to think of him.

"What else did he tell you?"

"He loves curry puffs," she said with sudden inspiration. "And he's crazy about satay with peanut sauce." All of which was true, but it certainly was not newly garnered information.

"Is that what you talked about with an interesting man? Food?" Nazirah's tone indicated a severe lack of admiration for this particular tactic.

"Food's a great subject," Nicky said brightly. "Everybody has to eat it. It's uncontroversial, but everybody has an opinion."

Nazirah rolled her eyes.

Nicky laughed. "You can learn a lot about people by finding out what kind of food they like. Whether they're adventurous, have imagination, are conservative, romantic, boring stick-in-the-muds. I did an article about how to use food in character analysis last month. I think I did my readers a great service."

"And what did you find out about him?" Nazirah asked doubtfully. "What kind of food does he like and what does it say about his character?"

"He likes everything," Nicky said casually, which was basically the truth. "Which makes him a conservative, imaginative adventurer with stick-in-the-mud tendencies."

Nazirah laughed. "And how does he do in the romance department?" Amusement glimmered in her blue eyes.

"Romance?"

"Is he a romantic?"

Nicky braced herself mentally. "He has his moments," she stated in a businesslike tone. "Flowers, chocolates, jewelry, that sort of thing." Sometimes luxury cookbooks, and odd knickknacks from exotic places in the world.

"Mmm. What about love letters and poetry? What about sexy phone calls?" Nazirah lowered her voice. "I *love* sexy phone calls."

Nicky's chest tightened and she swallowed at the sudden painful lump in her throat. She looked away. "Nope."

"Is he a good lover?"

Her heart turned over. Good God, she had to change the subject. The last thing she wanted to think about was Blake's talents in bed. "Listen," she said impatiently, "there are limits to what you can find out about a man by knowing his food preferences. If you're so interested in the man, go out with him, sleep with him and find out for yourself." *Good Lord*! she thought in a panic. *What am I saying*?

Nazirah stared at her. "Why are you mad at me?"

"I'm not mad at you." Nicky bit her tongue. Oh, God, she was giving herself away.

"Sure seems like it. I was just making conversation, having a little fun with this idea of yours."

"I'm sorry."

Nazirah was silent for a moment. "I'm not trying to make you angry, but if you're interested in him, I'll stay clear of him."

"I'm not interested in him. You can have him." Nicky heard the snappish tone of her own voice, took a deep breath, and forced a smile. "Maybe your mother can ask him to dinner. He loves home-cooked meals." She bit her lip. "He told me," she added.

Confusion, hesitation chased each other across Nazirah's face. "You know this man, don't you?" she asked softly.

"No," Nicky said, feeling herself turn cold. "I only thought I did."

*   *   *

She'd been twenty-one when she'd met Blake at a party given by her parents in Washington, D.C. At the time Blake worked with her father at USAID and her father thought the world of him. One look at Blake and Nicky had thought the world of him, as well. Her heart had nearly stopped and she'd almost forgotten to breathe. The world around her had ceased to exist. The glass of wine she'd had in her hand had slipped and fallen to the floor, the glass not breaking but the wine soaking irreverently into her mother's priceless Persian prayer rug.

Blake had found her another glass of wine and had not left her side for the rest of the evening. The days and weeks that followed had blurred into a whirlwind of love, laughter and passion.

She'd been in love plenty of times, but nothing compared to this. This was the real thing! She loved this man with all her soul. She knew it. Absolutely.

A month later they were married.

Nazirah stopped asking questions and for a while they drove on silently through the city and Nicky looked outside taking in the sights and the people.

She was in love with Kuala Lumpur, with its wonderful mixture of architecture illustrating the country's turbulent colonial history. Contemporary high rises blended in with Moorish mosques, Chinese temples and Victorian buildings left by British colonial rule. Lush tropical greenery shaded the roads and buildings.

Her stomach growled inelegantly and Nazirah grinned. "Didn't you have breakfast?"

"No. I didn't want to spoil my appetite." There'd be plenty of food to eat at the market, and Nicky was ready for some. It was only fair that if she was going to write about the food, she should try it first. She had her notebook and pen ready, as well as a good dose of enthusiasm to help her along. Open markets were her most

favorite places. She grinned at herself. It was going to
be an exciting day. She could feel it already.

Lighted minarets stood silhouetted against the dark night
sky like an image from the Arabian Nights as Nicky rode
home in a taxi that night. She felt exhausted but exhilarated, and she didn't think she was going to eat again
for a week.

The large gates stood open and the car drove noiselessly up the drive toward the front door of her father's
house. Nicky got out, paid the turbaned Sikh driver and
moved up the veranda steps. The night watchman lay
asleep on his mat and didn't stir as she let herself in.
Poor guy. He probably had a day job, as well, to make
ends meet.

The house was silent. Her father had flown to
Singapore for business and wouldn't be back until
sometime tomorrow. The house felt empty and lonely.
She sighed and turned on the brass table lamps in the
living room and dropped her notebook and purse amid
the silk embroidered cushions on the sofa. She might as
well work on her notes tonight, but first she'd get out
of her clothes and shower off the days' heat and dust.

Quickly she moved through the hall to her room,
opened the door, switched on the light and froze.

Her heart made a sickening lurch, then started racing
when a rush of adrenaline flooded her. Chaos. Drawers
had been turned over, clothes strewn everywhere. The
French windows stood wide open, the lacy white curtains wafting eerily in the breeze.

Never had anything like this happened to her before
and for an interminable moment her legs would not move
and she stood rooted to the floor, her heart pounding
like a sledgehammer.

Burglars, was her first thought. Burglars searching for
money, jewelry.

Jewelry! Her mother's diamond necklace! Oh, God, no! It was an heirloom, passed on from mother to daughter for several generations. She rushed over to the dresser, found the velvet jewelry bag emptied out on the top—her rings, earrings, her mother's necklace. It was all there. Nothing had been taken. Relief washed over her, then utter confusion. If the burglars hadn't wanted her jewelry, then what had they been looking for? The rest of the house had been untouched. Or at least the living room had appeared to be and that's where the TV was, and the VCR and the CD player.

What did they want in her room?

Her legs were trembling as she scanned the room, trying to see, to understand. *I've got to do something*, she thought. *I've got to call somebody. The police.* She reached for the bedside phone, realizing at the same time that 9-1-1 would do her no good outside the United States, that she didn't know the local emergency number, if there even was one.

She realized something else, as well. The phone was dead.

Never before had she known such fear.

And then it got worse.

Movement behind her. As she swung around, a hand clamped over her mouth and she was bodily lifted off the floor and carried out of the bedroom door.

CHAPTER TWO

PARALYZED by fear, Nicky felt herself being carried through the hall and living room and out the front door. She was gasping for breath as the two powerful arms that held her pressed her face forcefully against a hard chest. She started struggling, kicking her legs, but she was nothing more than a doll in the steely grip.

"Not a sound or we're both dead!" growled a low voice, the tone deadly and ominous. A voice intimately familiar.

Fear flooded out of her. "Blake?" she asked, but her voice was smothered by his chest, barely audible.

"Quiet!"

His chest was warm and solid against her face. For a fleeting moment she had an odd sense of déjà vu—as if once before she'd been carried off like this in the dark of night.

She heard the pumping of his heart against her cheek and her senses reeled with the familiar warm male scent of him, overwhelming for one delirious moment all other thought.

He pushed her almost roughly into the back seat of a car, slid in beside her, giving an order to the driver and before she could catch her breath they were tearing down the drive.

She was panting, her throat raw. "What the hell is this all about?" She struggled for the words, rubbing at a scratch on her arm where a branch had scraped the skin, her confusion greater than her fear now. They were in a taxi, she realized, and going at great speed.

"Be quiet," he said on a low note, warning in his voice. "Later." He glanced out the back window.

"Later what? Where are you taking me?" she demanded. "Are you insane, what is this all about?"

Steely eyes met hers. "I said be quiet." His voice was ominously low. "You'll be fine as long as you act normally."

She suppressed a hysterical little laugh. Sure, no sweat. She was used to being carried off into cars against her will. Of course she would act normally. "Are you out of your mind?" she whispered fiercely.

His silence was eloquent.

She hated his superior manner. She hated him. This, of course, was nothing new. She had entertained about this man every emotion known to mankind, except one: physical fear. And she wasn't afraid of him now, which, under the present circumstances, was something to be grateful for.

She closed her eyes and leaned back in the seat. Her whole body was trembling with shock and she felt the terrible urge to break down in tears or, alternatively, scream at Blake in fury. Her pride wouldn't allow her to do either.

Who was Blake to kidnap her out of her father's house? Why in the world would he want to? It didn't make sense. She thought of the ransacked room and shivered. Nothing made sense. She thought of her father, seeing again the worry edged in his face and her stomach twisted with anxiety. Something was wrong.

Something indeed was very wrong.

Could this possibly have something to do with that business deal he'd been having trouble with? *Unscrupulous*, he had called the Hong Kong company. It was not a nice word. In fact, it was a frightening word. She thought of her ravaged room and shivered again, her mind in chaos. But why would Blake be involved?

What could Blake possibly have to do with it? It was crazy; it made no sense at all.

Fear and anger fought for dominance in her mind. Why hadn't her father told her what was going on? Why was he always treating her as if she were a child who should not be bothered by her parents' problems? Well, she knew why. She was the baby of the family, and the only daughter. Her parents and three older brothers all had treated her like a princess, and although she wouldn't dare complain about the love and nurture she had received as a child, she wouldn't mind being respected as a mature adult now that she'd reached the ripe age of twenty-seven.

The car stopped and she opened her eyes. There were lights and people. More cars. People laughing. They were in front of what appeared to be a luxury hotel.

"Come along." Blake helped her out of the car, putting an arm around her when she almost lost her balance. His face was close to hers. "Don't do anything stupid," he said under his breath, apparently not wanting the driver to overhear him. "You're safe as long as you do what I say."

She stiffened. This was not the man she remembered. He had never ordered her around before, never told her what to do, never made any demands. He'd considered her an independent person who made her own choices and decisions. She wouldn't have wanted it any other way.

She felt dazed and disoriented. With his hand on her shoulder Blake propelled her through the cool, sumptuous hotel lobby. Crystal chandeliers, soft piano music, people in beautiful clothes, mingling, laughing. It all seemed to come from a distance, unreal. Then she found herself in a mirrored elevator.

Her reflection shocked her. She looked like a madwoman, her hair wild, her clothes dirty and sweaty from the day's exploration of the city's hot, crowded markets and streets. The elevator zoomed up, stopped. They got off. She moved as if in a trance, down a carpeted corridor, past endless doors. Blake stopped in front of one of the rooms and slid a small plastic card into a slot in the lock. The door open, he nudged her ahead of him into the room. She took in the big bed, the desk, a cozy seating arrangement near the window. Soft carpeting under her feet. Everything clean and comfortable.

She turned to face him, clenching her hands into fists by her side and anchoring her feet to the floor to keep them from trembling. "I want to know what this is all about!" she demanded, hearing an unfamiliar, shrill tone in her voice. Anger heated her blood and she could no longer contain it—anger mixed with a terrible fear, and other feelings she couldn't even begin to analyze. "What the hell is going on? Why did you bring me here?"

"Don't yell at me," he said coolly.

She almost stomped her foot. "I'll damn well yell if I want to! I'll scream!" She couldn't believe her own behavior. What possessed her? It was as if someone else had taken over, some wild creature driven in a corner, terrified and helpless.

"Calm down and we'll talk." He turned his back on her and picked up a bottle of Scotch standing on a tray on the dresser.

"*Calm down*?" she raged. "Are you out of your mind? You expect me to calm down after my room has been turned upside down and I've been kidnapped?"

"I did not kidnap you. I rescued you."

"*Rescued me*? From what? I want to know what's going on!"

He poured Scotch in two glasses. "I'll tell you what I know, but not until you get yourself under control."

She nearly choked on her words. "How dare you treat me this way!" she said to his back. "How dare you just carry me off! What's got into you? Are you the one who destroyed my room?" Even as she said it, she knew the idea was preposterous. Under no circumstances could she imagine Blake turning over drawers, going through closets. It didn't fit his code of ethics.

He turned and gave her a dark look. "No, I did not," he said sharply. "A couple of hired thugs from Hong Kong did. They were waiting in the bushes for you to come home and kidnap you. I thought I'd better beat them to it."

Her heart skidded to a stop, rushed on again in a frantic rhythm. Her knees buckled and she sat down on the edge of the big bed. Fear overtook her anger. "This is insane," she whispered. "Why?"

"After you left the party last night, I had another talk with your father. I gathered he unknowingly inherited a bad situation from his predecessor—an unfortunate business deal with a less than reputable firm in Hong Kong. They're running a scam and he's trying to back out of the contract. They're not very happy about it."

Her heart lurched. "I *knew* there was something wrong! He just didn't want to tell me. He kept saying it wasn't anything to worry about."

"Well, it was. More so than he suspected, I imagine. They wanted him to change his mind about breaking the contract. Apparently they thought kidnapping you might give him the right incentive."

"Oh, my God," she whispered.

He added ice to the glasses and handed her one. "Drink this. It will calm your nerves."

"I don't like whiskey," she said shakily.

"I know, but it's all I have." He gave her a wry smile. "I had not counted on entertaining my ex-wife in my hotel room tonight."

Certainly no signs of any such plans, she had to admit. No candles or flowers or champagne cooling in a bucket of ice. He hadn't touched her for his own selfish, carnal reasons—like a hero in a novel. A hero, who, seeing his old love unexpectedly at a party, was overwhelmed by remorse over the past and, gripped by new passion, had kidnapped her. That's only the way it went in stories. She was deranged even to have that fleeting thought.

He sat down in a chair and stretched out his legs. He was wearing gray slacks and a short-sleeved silk shirt, and did not look to be in the grip of passion. He looked exhausted, which was not surprising. Abduction was a tiring business, no doubt. Still, tired or not, he looked tough and masculine, and very sexy with his hair disheveled and his face full of dark shadows.

She sipped the whiskey, wincing, feeling the stuff burn down her throat.

"What kind of business deal was this?" she asked then.

He raked a weary hand through his hair. "An investment deal for the construction of an electronics plant in China. As I said, your father discovered that the Hong Kong firm was running a scam."

"So what is your part in all this, then?" It didn't make sense. Why should Blake be involved? He hadn't worked with her father for years. It was only coincidence they were in Malaysia at the same time.

His mouth curved down, as if he mocked himself. "I was the unfortunate bystander propelled into a rescue mission," he said dryly.

"Unfortunate bystander?" What was that supposed to mean?

He quirked a dark brow. "You don't think I went through this exercise just for the fun of it, do you?"

"No, of course not. Abducting your ex-wife to entertain her for the evening—what a nightmare of an idea."

He gave her an impenetrable look, saying nothing.

"So why did you do it?" she asked harshly. "Why not let them take me? Why did you care?" It was a bitchy, bitter question and she was sorry the moment the words were out. She was not a bitchy, bitter person. Oh, God, she sure hoped not.

He stared at her, a sudden, hot flash of anger in his eyes. "Oh," he answered coldly, "I always rescue maidens in distress. Besides, I found myself with nothing better to do for the evening."

The flash of anger disturbed her. He was a man of superb control, but her nasty remark had hit him wrong. She took another sip of the whiskey. The only way to drink the stuff was to consider it medicine and she felt in need of some sort of potion to stabilize her wrecked equilibrium.

"How did you know about all of this? I mean, if you're not involved."

He grimaced. "By sheer coincidence. I happened to overhear a conversation. I had trouble believing what I was hearing, but there was only one conclusion to be drawn." He shrugged and took a long drink from his whiskey.

"What conversation? Who was talking?"

"I was in a restaurant at the Hilton, waiting to meet a friend for dinner. He was late and two men at the next table were talking. I heard your father's name and consequently gave them my full attention, which was fortunate. They discussed their plans to have you escorted to Hong Kong tonight. Some hired help was going to do the honors. It seemed a good idea for me to abandon friend and dinner and to abort the gentlemen's plans if I wasn't too late already." He tossed back the last of his drink. "Just a cosmic little joke for me to overhear this," he finished derisively.

Characteristically, he'd told her the story in a few brief sentences. He'd never been a man of many words. He rubbed his neck. "We'd better call your father. He told me he'd be in Singapore tonight. Do you know which hotel he's staying at?"

"The Mandarin," she said, feeling numb. It was too much to grasp, this outrageous story. Not so outrageous. You read similar tales in the papers, heard them on TV. It just seemed crazy because it was happening to her. There was no reason to think Blake was lying. She finished the whiskey and put down the glass.

Blake had asked information for her father's hotel number and was dialing. He held out the receiver to her.

"You want to talk to him first?"

She shook her head. "You know what happened. You tell him." She listened as he told her father what had happened, assuring her father she was safely with him at the hotel. There was silence for a while.

"Yes, of course. No problem," Blake said. "Don't worry about it. I'll let you know." He handed the receiver to Nicky. "He wants to talk to you."

She took in a deep breath to steady herself.

"Hi, Dad."

"Thank God you're all right." His voice sounded rough with emotion. "I'll get the police on this immediately. I had no idea they'd go to these lengths, but they'll pay hell for this. I'll make sure of it."

"Who are these people doing this? What kind of people are they? Dad, I want you to tell me!"

"It's complicated, princess. I misjudged the seriousness of it, and if something would have happened to you I would never have forgiven myself."

Getting a clear answer was too much to hope for.

"I don't want anything to happen to you, either, Dad!" Again that shrill tone in her voice. "Please be careful!"

"Oh, I'll be careful. Don't you worry about me. But do me a favor. You've got to get out of town. Do what Blake tells you to do."

Do what Blake tells you to do. She would have laughed if she hadn't felt so shaky. Her father would trust Blake, of course. They'd worked together for five years and they'd always liked and respected each other. The divorce had not had her father's blessing.

"Nicky, promise me!"

"I can take care of myself, Dad!" It was an automatic response, and not a very smart one under the circumstances. She glanced over at Blake who'd poured himself another Scotch and was gazing out over the city, his back turned to her. Strong, straight shoulders, lean torso, long legs firmly planted on the floor. A man to reckon with. She closed her eyes briefly, hearing her father's voice over the phone.

"Nicky, I don't want to have to worry about you, do you understand?" His voice held command, but the underlying tension was audible. "I want to know you're safe!"

She swallowed a nervous little laugh. Safe. How safe was she in the presence of her ex-husband? How safe was she from her own tormented emotions?

"Nicky?" There was a desperate sound in her father's voice and her heart cringed. She closed her eyes.

"All right, Dad, if that's what you want." Her father had enough problems without having to worry about her.

He let out an audible sigh. "Good girl. Now I'd better call the police."

Good girl. She winced. Well, no matter.

Blake turned as she put the receiver down. "Got answers to your questions?" he asked.

"It wasn't what you'd call a very satisfactory conversation," she said irritably.

"This isn't a very satisfactory situation," he returned dryly.

He was probably as delighted to be here with her as she was to be here with him. "I'll have another drink," she said, and caught a sudden spark of humor in his eyes, gone in an instant. He poured her another measure of whiskey and handed it to her without comment.

"Thank you." She took a big gulp, wincing.

"Take it easy, Nicky," he said mildly.

In answer, she glared at him and took another swallow.

He picked up the menu. "This little adventure has left me ravenous," he commented. "I'll order us some dinner from room service. What would you like?"

She shook her head. "Nothing. I've eaten all day. I've been sampling street food for an article I'm writing." And even if she hadn't eaten all day, she couldn't imagine wanting anything now. She felt as if she were thrown into a nightmare and couldn't get out. She raked her hand through her hair. She felt dirty and sticky and she didn't even have a comb to fix her hair. She didn't even have her purse. It was sitting on the living room sofa on top of her notebook.

She felt naked without her purse—no identification, no money, no credit cards. The magnitude of her helplessness flooded through her like the heat of the whiskey. Oh, God, what was she going to do?

"What should I be doing now?" she asked, feeling like a helpless child, sitting there on the side of the bed, her hands clasped in her lap like a timid schoolgirl, and he, standing, towering over her. She wasn't used to asking anybody what to do. She was an independent, mature person and she usually knew what to do.

"Nothing, for the time being," he said, studying the room service menu. "Relax."

"*Relax*? Oh, sure, I'll relax," she said, trying to inject mockery into her tone, but it came out shakily, her voice trembling.

He glanced down at her face, and in the silence she glimpsed a softening in his eyes, a brief hesitation. He reached out and touched her cheek in a fleeting caress. "Everything will be all right, Nicky. You're safe. And your father knows how to take care of himself."

She dropped her gaze to her hands clenched in her lap. Her throat closed at the sudden gentleness in his voice, the touch of his warm hand on her cheek. She didn't want to feel this way, this yearning to be held by him, to find comfort from the fear that clutched at her heart.

She swallowed hard. "I have nothing with me," she said miserably. "No money, no clothes." She glanced up at him. "Would you mind getting me a room in this place so at least I can shower and sleep? Tomorrow I'll figure out what to do and pay you back."

"You're staying right here tonight," he said calmly. "We might have been followed here and I'm taking no risks with you in a room by yourself."

I don't want to be alone with you, came the automatic reply. But it stayed silent in her head. She fought to be calm and rational and not let her emotions create havoc.

"I'm not your responsibility," she said huskily. Her hands shook and she put the glass down.

His eyes held hers. "I'm making you my responsibility," he said with calm authority.

Her father had asked him to take care of her, no doubt. *Do what Blake tells you to do*, he'd told her. "I suppose my father asked you over the phone. You could have told him to figure out something else, you know."

He gave her an odd look. "There's not much I would not do for your father."

She stared at him. "What do you mean?"

His expression was a mingling of surprise and impatience. "Come on, Nicky, you know why. I admire and respect him." He hesitated for a moment. "He's been more of a father to me than my own ever was."

She felt a sudden constriction in her throat. "I didn't know you felt that way," she said.

Blake frowned. "How could you not know?" he asked.

She shrugged. "I . . . you never told me you felt about him that way."

She'd known they'd liked each other, of course. What she hadn't known was the extent of Blake's feelings for her father. Blake's own father had left him and his mother when Blake had been five. He'd seen him all of three times since.

She drained her glass. She was exhausted and her head felt dizzy with the whiskey. Her capacity for rational thought and decisive action was severely limited, so for the moment she had little choice but to go along with what Blake suggested.

He gestured to the bathroom door. "Have a shower. It will make you feel better. There's a bathrobe behind the door." He picked up the phone. "Are you sure you don't want something? A cup of mint tea with honey, maybe?"

Her heart made an odd little leap. She swallowed. "All right, yes. I'd like that." Mint tea, after all, was good for the digestion. She came to her feet and went into the bathroom, closing the door behind her. She leaned against the cool tile wall and took in a deep breath. So he remembered she liked mint tea with honey. What did that mean except that he had a good memory? They'd been married for two years. Surely he remembered things about her likes and disklikes. After all, didn't she remember plenty about him?

She stripped off her clothes, taking in the sumptuous bathroom, the marble floor, the thick fluffy towels and the array of luxury toiletries, compliments of the hotel.

She filled the tub and put in some fragrant bath oil. Why take a shower when she could have a leisurely bath? It would relax her; it always did.

Except this time. Her head was too full of fearful questions and nervous apprehension. Would her father really be all right? What about her being in this room tonight? She felt like a nervous wreck thinking about being alone with Blake.

Blake who was still the same, and yet so different. He was still the same utterly attractive man she had fallen in love with. He was also harder and colder. And the shine of laughter in his eyes was no longer there.

A knock came on the bathroom door and startled her. "Your tea is here. You want it in there?"

Her pulse leapt. "No, thanks. I'll be out in a minute."

She let the tub drain, turned on the shower and shampooed her hair and rinsed off. It was good to feel clean again. The huge towel felt soft and luxurious. She wrapped another towel around her wet hair and pulled on one of the two hotel robes behind the door. Bundling up her clothes, she went back into the bedroom.

"Do you think we can get these washed by tomorrow morning?" she asked.

He glanced up from his newspaper. "Sure." He reached for the phone. "Anything else you need? A toothbrush?"

She nodded. "Please." She sat down at the table and poured the tea from a small pot and stirred in some honey while Blake was on the phone. Her body felt tense, her nerves frayed. She sipped the hot tea, surveying the dishes on the table, as yet covered and untouched. He had waited for her before eating. Always the gentleman.

She moaned inwardly. Oh, God, she didn't want to think about the past, about what had been.

He put the phone down and sat across from her at the table and took the covers off the plates, exposing an Oriental noodle dish with huge shrimp and a salad.

"It looks good," she said for something to say.

"You can have some if you like."

"No, thanks." She sipped the fragrant tea. "You remembered I like mint tea," she heard herself say.

His eyes met hers across the table. "Of course I do, Nicky," he said, his mouth twisting in an odd little smile. "Why wouldn't I?"

She shrugged uneasily. "I don't know, I just..." Her voice faltered. "I just didn't think it would be something you'd remember."

"I remember a lot. More than is comfortable." He picked up fork and glanced down at his food.

Her heart contracted. She remembered, too, and it certainly wasn't comfortable. She stared into her cup, wondering about the sleeping arrangements, what he had in mind. There was only the one bed, king-size as it might be. They could easily sleep in it together and never know the other one was in it.

Sure, sure. She closed her eyes and swallowed more tea. She could suggest she sleep on the floor, or in one of the chairs. He wouldn't let her. She knew him well enough. There was something terribly unreal about this situation.

"You look tired," he said, surveying her face.

"I am. I was on my feet practically all day."

"Tell me about your article."

So she did, feeling relieved to have her thoughts distracted. "Have you ever eaten snake?" she asked, remembering seeing the creatures for sale in the market that morning—a lifetime ago.

"Tastes like chicken. Quite good."

She grimaced. "It's all in my head, I know, but I'm not ready for that adventure."

Blake had finished his food and leaned back in his chair, only to come to his feet again when a knock came on the door. A smiling maid stated she had come to pick up the laundry. She had barely left when another one delivered a toothbrush.

As he once more closed and locked the door, Blake tossed Nicky the toothbrush. "If you want to go to sleep, go ahead. Would it bother you if I watched the news on TV for a while? I'll turn it low."

"No, of course not." It was, after all, his room. "Where do you want me to sleep?" she asked.

He raised a dark brow. "In the bed, of course."

"And you?"

"In the bed, too. Where else? Plenty of space. I'm sure we can manage. We have done this before, remember?"

Her heart lurched. "That was quite a while ago." She sounded nervous. "And we were married."

He gave her an impenetrable look. "Don't stand there like a frightened virgin, for God's sake. Don't worry, I won't force myself on you. I never have and I won't now."

Heat washed over her—a rush of anger, of memories, of embarrassment. No, he had never forced himself on her. All he had to do was smile his special smile, touch her softly, kiss her—anything at all and she was instantly aflame. Oh, God, she did not know if she would survive the night with him next to her in bed. She forced herself to be calm.

"Good," she said tightly. "I'll dry my hair and brush my teeth."

"There's toothpaste in my toiletry kit, and dental floss. Help yourself." So cool, so calm.

"Thank you." She swung around and went into the bathroom, feeling her legs trembling. She saw herself in the mirror, flushed, her eyes bright. A nervous virgin. She was pathetic!

She gritted her teeth, dragged the towel from her head and reached for the dryer mounted to the wall. She switched it on full, using her fingers to comb through her hair and lift it to dry it, the noise of the dryer an odd comfort. Her chest felt tight and for a terrible moment she was afraid she might break out in tears for a reason she couldn't even fathom. Concentrating on the whining noise of the hair-dryer, she managed to control herself and the moment passed.

Her hair was very short and naturally curly and it didn't take long to dry. She took the toothbrush from its box and looked around to locate Blake's black leather toiletry kit, the same functional model he'd had years ago, but probably a newer version. A hairbrush lay beside it. Hesitating, she picked it up and used it to give her hair a quick going over now that it was dry.

The toiletry kit stood open and she took out the toothpaste and brushed her teeth, then searched for the small box of floss. It seemed to be an oddly intimate thing to be going through his kit, but he'd told her to do it. There was nothing but the usual stuff inside—a razor, a can of shaving foam, antiperspirant, aspirin, some first aid cream, his toothbrush and the dental floss. She took it out, cut off a piece and tossed the box back into the kit.

Back in the room she found Blake watching CNN, his shoes and socks off, bare feet propped up on the bed. Even his feet still looked familiar. She'd be able to pick them out of a thousand other pairs.

She stood in front of the bed, hesitating. Now, she could casually take off the bathrobe and slide between the sheets, but it was more than she was prepared to do with him having a front row seat for the show. When they'd been married she'd never worn anything to bed, but they were no longer married and if she was going to sleep in the same bed with him she was damn well going to wear something.

"Do you have something I can sleep in?" she asked. "A T-shirt?"

He gazed at her for a moment, as if her simple request needed digesting. Then he gestured at the dresser. "Second drawer on the right. The blue one is good and long."

Was he making fun of her? She couldn't tell. She found the T-shirt, went back into the bathroom and pulled it on. It was a good thing he was big and she was so small. The T-shirt reached almost mid-thigh.

"Charming," he commented as she came back into the room. There was unexpected humor in his voice. "Do you honestly think that thing is going to keep me from ravishing you if I felt so inclined?"

"Oh, shut up," she snapped.

He laughed. "Go to sleep, woman, you're overwrought."

It was easier said than done. The bed was comfortable, the sheets cool and crisp, but her body was tense. She listened to the soft murmur of the television. It seemed ages before he turned it off. Had he been waiting for her to be asleep before coming to bed? She heard him move around, go into the bathroom, heard the shower running.

She pictured him standing in the falling water, naked, wet, soapy, bubbles clinging to the hair on his chest. It was so easy to visualize. She knew everything about that body, the way it felt pressed intimately against hers. A wave of memories washed over her and her body reacted with treacherous need.

Her heart pounding, she jerked upright in bed.

This was crazy. She was crazy. She could not stay here. She should call someone. Who? She didn't even have any clothes to put on. Oh, God, this was like a bad movie.

The shower was turned off. She scooted back under the covers, eyes closed, body rigid. He was drying himself off, wiping his face, his chest. He was brushing his teeth.

Stop it! Stop it!

The door opened quietly. Footsteps came softly toward the bed. She felt his weight on the mattress, the movements of his body as he made himself comfortable on the other side, heard the click of the lamp as he turned it off.

Silence, punctuated by the throbbing of her heart. She opened her eyes and stared into the darkness, afraid to move, afraid to breathe. After a while she heard Blake's slow, regular breathing. He was asleep.

She felt an unreasonable, bitter anger. Here he was, asleep, not bothered at all by her being in his bed.

Well, why should he? They'd been married once, but that was over now. He'd probably had ten women since her.

She didn't want him if he begged her. The thought almost made her laugh out loud. Blake never begged for anything.

She was floating in crystal blue water and the sky bloomed in soft pastels, greeting the rising sun. So beautiful—she sighed with the wonder of it. Gentle waves lapped sensuously against her skin, taking her back to the beach, back to Blake who was waiting for her to come to him.

Pink sand. So beautiful. So soft. She lay down and stretched out her arms to touch the warmth, to touch Blake, pleasure curling languorously through her body.

He felt warm and solid and she snuggled closer against him, his breath brushing her face. The sun rose higher and higher, the air grew hotter and hotter. She murmured his name, breathing in the familiar scent of him, her body flooding with trembling need, wanting him, wanting him.

Trembling need. Dizzying hunger. And an aching sadness. Her fingers tangled in his thick hair, slipped down his neck to his back. It was smooth and strong under her hands. She shifted a little, searching for his mouth, kissing him, hearing the soft groan coming from deep inside him.

It was so wonderful to kiss him, to feel the sweet, seductive yearning. So why this sadness? The soundless tears? As if she knew she would never have what she so desperately craved. As if all of this was just a fragile illusion.

His heart beat against hers. She could feel it against her breast, hear it. So wonderful. Two hearts beating together. She clung to him, closer still, her arms around him. Comfort and bliss. She fought the sadness, wanting only to feel the magic of their bodies together. "Hold me," she whispered. "Make love to me."

"Nicky?" A sound from another world, harsh, tortured.

She felt dragged into consciousness, heart racing, darkness everywhere. She gulped in air, disoriented, feeling the roughness of an unshaven chin, the warm skin of a naked body intimately close against her.

Light flooded the room, and she found herself staring into Blake's smoke-gray eyes. Oh, God, she thought, freezing over. I don't believe this.

CHAPTER THREE

SHE was over on his side of the bed, intimately nestled against his naked body—an intimacy that left no secrets hidden. She tore herself away. "I...you woke me up," she muttered inanely.

"Sweetheart, you woke me up," he said wryly. "Too bad. I was quite enjoying it."

She'd noticed. "I must have been having a nightmare," she returned, mortified. "You, in my bed."

He laughed softly. "Some nightmare. You were kissing me and touching me with quite some passion."

"I was dreaming of someone else." She didn't know where she got the presence of mind to come up with that one.

"I thought you said it was a nightmare. Are you trying to confuse me?"

As if there were even the faintest possibility that she could. She grasped the sheet, her hands clenched into fists. "I don't remember! I have no idea what I was dreaming or doing. I was *sleeping*! And then you woke me up!"

He braced his elbow against the mattress and propped his head up on his hand. He observed her with maddening calm. "Right. I apologize. I should have let you finish your...eh, dream."

"Why didn't you, if you so enjoyed it?"

His mouth curved. "I *am* capable of controlling my baser animal instincts."

"You never did before!"

"I never *had* to before—with you." Faint amusement in his voice.

"And why did you now?"

He shrugged. "This was different."

"So what was different? Why not have a little bonus of free sex?" She didn't like the way she sounded—the sharp, cynical edge to her voice. It wasn't her, not really.

One dark eyebrow quirked up. "It was different, for one thing, because you used to be fully conscious, well, most of the time. When you weren't I could be assured you wouldn't regret it later, since you, as my loving wife, were willing and wanting any time, anywhere."

She didn't know why this should make her feel embarrassed or humiliated, but it did. "You make it sound as if I were some kind of nymphomaniac! You'd be gone for weeks on end! Wasn't I supposed to want you when you came home?"

He gave a crooked smile. "I'd have been very disappointed if you hadn't."

He was making fun of her. She hated him. He was so in control of himself. Always in control. She couldn't stand it. Always calm and confident. He did not lose his temper. He seldom got angry. He never complained.

"Complaining is a sign of weakness," he'd once told her. "If you don't like something, either accept it and go on with your life or do something about it, take action. Don't waste time moaning about it."

She'd taken this bit of wisdom to heart and vowed not to be a moaning, complaining wife. Not much good it had done her. It was an unhappy thought. Not that she was complaining, of course.

She moved over further to the very edge of the mattress, feeling the T-shirt twisted up around her waist. She yanked it down as she struggled out of bed. It was four-thirteen, she read on the digital clock next to the bed. In the bathroom she drank a glass of water, wishing she could just walk out of the place, away from Blake, away from the nightmare of being with him again. Her eyes in the mirror looked dark and huge in her pale face.

How could this possibly have happened? How could she still feel like this about him after all these years, knowing it was useless, knowing he could never give her what she really needed . . .

She closed her eyes, feeling tears burn behind her lids, seeing his face, the humor in his eyes. Maybe it would have been better if he hadn't controlled himself, if they had made love. Then at least she could have had the comfort of not having been the only one losing control.

She groaned inwardly. What was she thinking!

A knock on the door. "Nicky?" Blake's voice, low but insistent.

"Go away," she said thickly, remembering she hadn't locked the door. "Leave me alone."

He opened the door. He had a *kain* wrapped around his waist, a sarong with colorful stripes. "Come back to bed."

She blinked away the tears. "Don't come barging in here!"

"Just making sure you're not trying to sleep in the tub," he said casually. "You can have the bed. I'll do some work. I'm usually up early anyway."

She knew that. She knew too damn much for her own comfort. She stared down at her hands gripping the cold edge of the sink, gathering her composure. She raised her head and looked at him. "All right, thank you." Spoken like a lady. She was proud of herself.

Nothing more was said. She slid back into bed, and he sat at the desk and began to type on his laptop computer. The staccato rhythm was oddly relaxing—a dry click-clack that had nothing to do with emotion and desire.

Bright sunlight awoke her, streaming over her face and body. She struggled against it briefly, turning around and burying her face in the pillow. But consciousness claimed her and with it the knowledge of reality. She lay still and opened her eyes. Blake had pulled back the curtains, and was pouring coffee at the small room-service table that must have been wheeled in while she was still asleep. She'd been dead to the world.

He had shaved and dressed, was no longer wearing the colorful *kain* wrapped around his hips. Thank God. The last thing she wanted now was to look at that strong, tanned chest with its light covering of dark hair, imagining all manner of things. He wore sand-colored cotton Dockers and a deep blue polo shirt—simple, comfortable clothes without pretense. Of course, with a man like Blake, no pretense was necessary: his masculinity needed no help from expensive clothes or practised behavior. It was there naturally, coming from the inside, from a deep core of strength.

He moved over to the bed and she closed her eyes. He sat down on the edge beside her. She smelled the faint, clean scent of soap and after-shave.

"Nicky? Wake up."

She had no choice but to open her eyes and see him looking down at her, his face too close for comfort. She could see the silvery flecks in his gray eyes, the small lines fanning out at the corners of his eyes.

"I'm awake," she said, her voice husky. She felt overwhelmed with his nearness—his sheer male energy charging the air around her. She felt the tingle of it on her skin, felt it skittering through her body.

"Here's some coffee." His voice was even.

She sat up and glanced at the cup he was offering her. *Café au lait*. Strong and milky, the way she liked it.

She took the cup from him. "Thank you."

He'd always been the early riser, she the late one. He'd always brought her coffee in bed, after he'd been up already, reading the paper, running, working.

It wasn't quite the same now as it had been. In the past he wouldn't just say her name to wake her. He'd kiss her awake—fluttery kisses on her closed eyelids, her mouth. Had he remembered, too? She saw his face, the dark glitter of emotion in his eyes and for a moment time stood still.

He remembered.

Of course he remembered. But what did that matter now? She pushed the memory away, and took a sip of the hot coffee.

"It's good," she said, trying to sound cool, breaking the spell.

He stood up from the bed, a shuttered look in his eyes now, his face unreadable. "Breakfast is on the table. Croissants and rolls, and some fruit. I assumed that's all you wanted."

"Yes. I'll get washed up."

"There's no hurry. Finish your coffee first, if you like." She watched him move away from her, taking in the easy movement of his body. He picked up a newspaper and sat down, feet propped up on the bed again.

She drank the coffee, listening to the silence, the restless drumming of her heart, the rustle of the paper. His face was hidden. In a way this was all so comfortable and familiar, yet at the same time so nerve-racking and strange. She finished the coffee and slipped out of the bed. He glanced up and waved at a chair.

"Your clothes are there."

"I can't believe I slept through all those comings and goings." She frowned. "I didn't hear a thing."

"You were always a deep sleeper," he commented. "It would be thundering and lightening and you wouldn't stir. Ambulances screaming down the street and you'd turn over and go right back.''

She grimaced. "Proof of a clear conscience, you used to say.''

He met her eyes. "You still have that, then?''

Her heart turned over. "What do you mean with that?''

He shook his head. "Nothing. Just making conversation.'' He folded the paper.

"Why wouldn't I have a clear conscience?'' she persisted, feeling anger rise. "What are you hinting at?''

He gave a light shrug. "Haven't seen you for a long time. Who knows, the FBI may be hunting for you all over creation.'' He put the paper down and came to his feet. "Shall I pour you more coffee?'' His face was neutral, his voice polite.

She stared at him angrily, knowing full well that she wasn't going to get a better answer out of him. "I don't like insinuations,'' she said. "And no, I don't want coffee now. I'll get dressed first.''

She took her things and went into the bathroom. What had he insinuated with his question? She had no idea. She shrugged as she splashed water over her face. Examining the moisturizing cream supplied by the hotel, she realized it was all she would have to put on her face. Oh, well, she didn't care. There was nobody she needed to impress with an immaculately made-up face. She used Blake's brush again to do her hair, grateful she didn't need anything else to make it presentable.

They had breakfast at the small table, saying little, the silence uncomfortable. She felt frayed around the edges.

"I need to find a way to get my purse and papers, and some clothes,'' she said.

"We're staying away from the house. You'll have to do without.'' He buttered a roll and didn't look at her.

"I *can't* do without!" she said tightly. "I think that under the circumstances I'd better get on a plane and go back to the States."

"You'd never make it to the airport. It's too risky right now." He drained his coffee and filled the cup again.

She stabbed a piece of papaya with her fork. "And what am I supposed to be doing? Hide out here with you? Without clothes and money?" It was a nightmare not to be contemplated.

"No," he said coolly. "We'd better get out of town before they figure out I took you and where to find you." The words, calmly spoken, struck a cord of fear in her. She felt a shiver go down her back.

"If you're trying to frighten me, you're very successful."

"Good. Then stop worrying about clothes, for God's sake, and do what I say."

Do what Blake tells you. Her father's voice rang in her ears.

"You can't order me around!" she said furiously.

"Of course I can." A fleeting smile quirked his mouth. "I know how hard this must be for you to admit, but you need me. Think about your father. All he wants is assurance that his only daughter is safe."

"And I'm safe with you?" she asked bitterly.

"Are you afraid of me?" he asked, eyebrows arched.

Yes, she thought. She was afraid of him, of the impact his presence had on her, of the emotions being stirred up, but she could hardly tell him that, could she? She straightened her back.

"Of course not," she said tightly. "I don't imagine you have plans to lock me up in some dank cellar until such time you think all danger of kidnapping has passed."

"No. I have a better idea." He took a bite from his roll, which prevented him from saying more for the moment. She gritted her teeth as she watched him chew.

"Would you like to clarify that?" she asked when he swallowed.

"I'd be delighted to. What we're going to do is this... Friends of mine, John and Lisette O'Connor, have a house in the mountains, about four hours out of town. They're out of the country at the moment, but I made arrangements with them to stay at their house to write my report. It's pretty isolated and we can stay there until it's safe to go back to KL or until we find a way to get you out of the country."

"How?"

"I don't know yet. Maybe we can drive across the border into Thailand. Or maybe we can get you to a smaller airport and you can catch a domestic flight to Sarawak, Borneo, and get into Indonesia from there. We'll have to check out the possib—" He stopped midsentence. Then swore under his breath. "Those thugs turned your room upside down to find your passport," he stated with frigid finality.

"It wasn't in my room!" she said quickly, relief flooding her. "It's in my desk drawer at my father's office. He gave me a desk and a computer so I could work on my writing there. It's in there with my disks and my return ticket and some traveler's checks."

He let out a long sigh of relief. "Good." He raked his hand through his hair. "Well, we'd better get going then. I'll get packed."

"Do you have a car here?" she asked, remembering they'd come to the hotel in a taxi last night.

He tossed a suitcase onto the bed. "I can use the O'Connors'. It's parked at the house of friends of theirs here in town. They always keep it in KL when they're

leaving the country so they have it when they get back."
He opened drawers and began pulling out clothes.

A driver delivered the car to the hotel fifteen minutes
later. It was a rugged four-wheel drive Toyota Land
Cruiser, considerably battered and obviously well-used.

They drove in silence. Blake had never been given to
small talk. Even during their marriage he'd done little
talking. She had usually been the one to begin conver-
sations and to keep them going. The strong, silent type
he was. She'd been enamored by it then, found it sexy
and exciting, wondering what lay behind that quiet
facade, what fascinating thoughts lurked behind those
calm gray eyes.

Later it had no longer been exciting. She had silently
prayed for him to talk, to say the things she so desperately needed to hear. Instead, there had been silence, or
words that had not mattered.

She sensed the old bitterness stirring in her again and
tried to push it out. It was all in the past now.

Only he was sitting next to her again, now, in the
present. She bit her lip and focused on the scenery
outside. They' d left the city and were driving through
rural country past rubber plantations and picturesque
Malay villages. The wooden houses were built on stilts,
their thatched roofs shaded by tall coconut palms. In
the distance, misty, forest-covered hills reared up against
a deep blue sky.

"Tell me about your friends," she asked at last, "the
ones who own the house. Are they American?"

"John's American, Lisette is French. He's a botanist
and she's a nature photographer and they're both deep
into conservation issues."

"Why are they out of the country?"

"They're on a lecturing tour through the States.
They've been all over the Peninsula and Sarawak cata-
loging rain forest plants."

"Do they have kids?" She couldn't imagine how they'd manage the needs of a family.

"Two grown daughters. They're in the States."

"They're older than you, then, I guess." She felt as if she were doing an interview rather than having a conversation.

He shrugged indifferently. "In their early fifties."

"They must be interesting people. Do you see them often?"

"A couple of times a year. When I'm in the Far East I usually go up there to write my reports and spend a little time with them. I'm sorry to miss them this time."

There was silence again. Outside, they passed by rolling green valleys and hills, cultivated with shimmering green bushes—tea, she knew—and through Chinese villages where small shop houses spilled their goods onto the sidewalk. Above the shops were the living quarters—potted plants on the balconies, washing hanging from lines to dry. The different ethnic groups making up Malaysia's population made for a colorful and interesting country.

Blake was preoccupied, not making an effort at conversation. She studied his inscrutable face, wondering what he was thinking. He hadn't counted on her being with him and she wondered if he resented her presence. It was an uncomfortable thought.

"I'm sorry I'm causing you a problem," she said. "You hadn't counted on my coming with you."

"It's not a problem." His eyes met hers briefly. "Unless we make it a problem," he added.

"What do you mean?"

He shrugged lightly. "We are not exactly strangers to each other, and unfortunately our past relationship did not have a very satisfactory ending."

"That was a long time ago," she said tightly. "And I have no intention of making it a problem."

"Good. Neither do I."

She thought of waking up in his arms early that morning, snuggled tightly up against him, and she suppressed a wave of hot embarrassment. That had been a problem. A serious one.

They had lunch in a Malay village an hour later, eating *nasi lemak*, spicy coconut rice with fish, egg and cucumber wrapped up in a banana leaf. They ate it with their fingers, Malay style, and she was mentally writing up the experience of sitting here in this picturesque village with small children staring at them curiously and women draped head to foot in Muslim dress on their way to the small mosque for their midday prayers. She concentrated on taking in details, color—the dog sleeping in the shade under a house, the beautifully carved verandas of some of the houses.

"Here," she heard Blake say. She glanced at the small notebook and pen he slid over to her across the wooden table. She met his gaze, saw the faintly amused curve of his mouth.

"Thank you." She gave a half smile. "Can't resist."

"I know." There was unexpected warmth in his voice. "I can see it in your face—you get that certain look in your eyes."

She wiped her hands on a thin paper napkin, glad to have something to do, feeling oddly touched by his gesture and the tone of his voice. She began to write, recording her impressions to be worked out later, hoping that her notebook at home would still be there and not get lost somehow. Surely her father or the housekeeper would have found her purse and notes and keep them safe. She'd planned to work out the notes on the computer in her father's comfortable, air-conditioned office today. Instead she was here with her ex-husband in a Malay village hours out of town, eating food from a banana leaf, with nothing more in her possession than the clothes on her back.

She put the pen down. "I know you don't care to hear me talk about clothes," she began carefully, "but the reality is that I'll need something besides what I'm wearing now. Isn't there—"

"There'll be stuff at the house you can borrow. I'm sure Lisette won't mind."

"But I do." She didn't even know the woman. "A T-shirt or a pair of jeans, fine, but I draw the line at wearing someone else's underwear."

He gave a low laugh at that. "All right, all right. I imagine there's a market here somewhere."

The waitress told them yes, there was a *pasar*, in session today, down the road a little farther. Blake paid for their lunch and they got back in the Land Cruiser.

Nicky realized that she'd have to ask Blake for some money, as if she weren't dependent on him enough. The irony of the situation did not escape her. She clenched her teeth and stared ahead at the road. Oh, damn.

He gave her a quick sideways glance. "What's the matter?"

"I have no money." She sighed. "Would you mind lending me some?"

He glanced at her again, one eyebrow arched. "You look as if it's distasteful to ask."

"I don't like borrowing money!" she said tightly.

"Especially not from your ex-husband," he added dryly.

"Right." She wished it didn't bother her, but it did.

"Considering the circumstances, I wouldn't make a big deal out of it," he said evenly. "I don't mind in the least lending you some money."

"I'll pay you back," she said for good measure.

He rolled his eyes. "And please don't forget," he returned solemnly.

"I don't like feeling so dependent, dammit!" she snapped, knowing he was making fun of her. "You know that."

"Oh, yes, I know that. But we're only talking about some underwear and it's only me, your ex-husband. I don't believe I've ever been a threat to your independence."

No, he hadn't been. Whatever vices she could accuse him of, that wasn't one of them. He'd left her as free as a bird in the sky.

Too free, came the sudden, surprising thought. She shook it away impatiently. No one was ever too free.

One hand on the steering wheel, Blake fished his wallet out of his back pocket with the other and tossed it into her lap. "Take what you want."

It felt odd to have his wallet in her hands, the leather warm from his body. Yesterday she'd gone through his toiletry kit, used his toothpaste, brushed her hair with his brush. Now he told her to take money out of his wallet. Intimacies that should no longer belong between them, should no longer be appropriate.

She stared at the credit cards, the bills tucked in behind—dollars, as well as ringgit. There was plenty of money there. She took some of the bills and handed back the wallet.

He glanced at her. "You have enough?"

"I took a hundred ringgit." About thirty dollars.

They found the busy open market offering a wide variety of goods—food, charcoal, plastic toys, *batek* cloth, herbal medicines, and a stall full of ladies' and children's lingerie. Lacy bras, girls' flowered panties, embroidered nightgowns, silky seductive women's panties as well as sturdy, functional cotton ones made in China.

She selected some functional, white cotton ones, with Blake looking on, brows quirked sardonically. It wasn't what she was used to wearing and he knew it. She gave him a challenging look. "I've always had this fantasy of wearing Chinese underwear, so how can I pass up this opportunity?"

"I wouldn't want you to," he said mockingly. "Get a bra to match."

"I'll manage with the one I have." She could always go without. She couldn't buy a bra without trying it on to make sure it would fit.

She paid for the panties, then moved on and bought a comb and brush and a pair of flip-flops. She hesitated at a stall full of colorful *batek*-cloth sarongs, but Blake put a hand briefly on her shoulder.

"There are plenty of *kains* at the house."

She moved on to the food section. Women sat on mats with their wares in front of them, colorful piles of fragrant mangoes, ripe tomatoes, guavas, papaws and all sorts of other exotic fruit. She was admiring a bunch of *rambutan*, small round fruit with red hairy fibers, clustered on a stalk like hairy grapes.

"I love these things," she said to Blake. "Don't they look lethal with all those red fibers sticking out all over?"

"Yes, I suppose." He pushed his hands in his pockets and rocked back on his heels, scowling.

"Do you like them?"

"Yes," he said impatiently.

"Let's get some to eat in the car," she suggested.

"Fine." He turned to the market lady. "*Berapa ini?*" he asked, fishing some coins out of his pocket. When she answered him, he countered with another offer and handed her some money. She accepted without further bargaining. He picked up the stalk of rambutan. "Let's go," he ordered.

"Why? We haven't seen it all yet. Are we in a hurry?"

He gave an exasperated sigh. "You and markets. I should have known."

She stopped walking and faced him squarely. "I happen to love markets, especially the food sections, and if I remember correctly, you enjoyed them, too." They'd spent happy hours wandering through open markets, at home, on the Caribbean island where they'd spent their honeymoon, and in Venice, Italy, once.

His eyes had an odd shuttered look in them. "That was then and this is now. I'm not on vacation. I have no time for lollygagging and admiring ginger root."

She refused to move and stared back at him. "Are we in a hurry for something? Does fifteen minutes make a difference? You used to *like* this sort of thing."

"Well, I don't now," he said brusquely, and turned around, marching out of the market.

She wondered what she had done to annoy him. He'd never been a moody man. As a matter of fact, he'd been one of the more even-tempered people she'd ever known. He'd once told her that there were very few things in life he considered worthy of getting worked up about.

He was worked up now.

She stared at his retreating back, a faint suspicion whispering through her thoughts. Anger was often used as a cover for other emotions. Maybe he didn't like remembering what they had used to do together. Maybe the memories hurt him, as they hurt her. She sighed and followed him back to the car. She was imagining things.

They drove on in silence and her mind produced a memory of the week they'd spent in Italy, of the huge marketplace in Venice. He had been on his way to Africa to work, she to visit her friend Sophie who lived in Rome.

A wonderful market. It had been fall and there'd been countless stalls full of mushrooms—all kinds, small ones and big ones as large as a man's hand. She had never seen anything like it and she'd been enthralled.

She'd noticed Blake watching her with an amused grin. "What's so funny?" she'd asked.

"What I like about you is your enthusiasm. I've never known a person who got lyrical about smelly fungi."

She'd got quite indignant and he had laughed and hugged her, much to the approval of the Italian mushroom vendors.

"Don't ever change," he'd said in her ear.

They drove on through spectacular scenery—green mountains, shaded valleys. The air grew cooler still, the traffic lighter, the villages smaller. They passed flourishing market gardens where vegetables and fruit grew lusciously in the cool mountain air. A resort hotel sprawled on a hilltop. *Paradise Mountain Resort*, the sign read. It catered to tourists and the well-to-do from KL who needed a vacation and a respite from the humid tropical weather on the coast, Blake told her. Beautiful private homes lay half hidden in the greenery on the mountain slopes.

Half an hour later they passed through one more small *kampung* when the pavement stopped abruptly and changed into a rough track winding further up the mountain. All she saw around them now was dense jungle hugging the track, ready to claim it again. The sky was invisible, as the massive trees formed a dense canopy closing like a cathedral roof over the narrow road.

"How much longer?" she asked. Jostling around in this vehicle was no pleasure trip. She held on to the door.

"About twenty minutes."

"Good Lord, they live isolated. Don't they get lonely?"

He shrugged. "No. They're busy people, and they often have university students living with them, and conservation people. They are no recluses, believe me."

Nicky studied the jungle all around them, wondering what kind of place it was these people lived in. Some sort of primitive research camp? No plumbing. Washing in the river. Kerosene lamps. Cooking over open fires. She'd seen documentaries on television. Well, it would be an adventure.

"What kind of place is that house? I don't suppose there's electricity and water?"

"There's a generator, and they have their own water well. It's quite civilized. You'll like the place."

Okay, so no washing in the river and no kerosene lamps. Although it might seem a romantic vision, she wasn't too sorry to give it up.

Sky, sunlight, open space appeared in front of them suddenly, and in the middle of it, a large wooden house built on stilts Malay-style. It had a thatch roof and a veranda on the front and sides. The forest had made way for a beautiful garden with shade trees and blooming bushes and plants—a riot of color to please the spirit.

It was magical—like an oasis of sun and light in the dark forest. Nicky fell in love with the place instantly.

A gardener was busy trimming and clipping, and stopped his activities as Blake drove up to the front of the house. The man smiled and gave a wave of his hand, then went back to work.

"His name is Ali," said Blake, "and he's married to Ramyah, the housekeeper."

A slim Malay woman in a sarong and blue blouse came out of the door and down the veranda steps as Nicky clambered out of the vehicle. Blake smiled at her and spoke to her briefly in Malay. Nicky noticed she looked nervous, almost frightened.

Blake made introductions. Ramyah gave her a shy, polite smile, then turned and quickly moved back up the stairs.

"Is something wrong?" Nicky asked Blake.

He frowned. "I have no idea, but she sure doesn't act like her normal self."

"Did she know we were coming?"

"Yes. She knew I was coming, anyway, and there are people here all the time. That's not it." He shrugged. "I'll see what I can find out, but let's get you settled first."

They climbed up the wooden stairs, Blake carrying his suitcase. The door opened straight into a cool, spacious living room sporting casual rattan furniture chosen for comfort and an easy-going decor. There was no ceiling and she could see right up into the thatch-covered rafters. It was a place to feel comfortable in, to live in. On the far end of the room, large open doors led out onto another part of the veranda that encircled the house. It had a dramatic view of the forested mountains all around.

Blake showed her to a guest bedroom furnished in the same casual style, with a brightly colored woven bedspread and some blown-up photographs of jungle creatures on the wall.

"I'll ask Ramyah to find you some clothes," he said, and left her.

She surveyed her surroundings, not knowing what to do. All she had was the things she had bought in the market. She put them on the bed and just as she was about to go back to the living room, Ramyah appeared in the doorway with an armful of clothes.

"You try," she suggested, and put them on the bed.

The owner of the clothes obviously went for comfort rather than fashion, which was no problem as far as Nicky was concerned. She would manage fine with the sweat suits, the T-shirts and cotton slacks and shorts. For a few days, at least.

A few days alone with Blake. Anxiety churned inside her. She took a ragged breath and closed her eyes.

When she opened them again, she found Blake standing in the open door, glancing at the clothes on the bed. "Did you find something?" he asked.

"This will be fine. Nice and serviceable stuff."

His mouth twitched. "Will go nicely with the Chinese lingerie."

"Who cares," she said coolly. "I'm not here on my honeymoon." Oh, God, what a thing to say. What kind of Freudian twist of the mind had made her say that?

He leaned against the doorjamb, hands in his pockets, all casual male confidence. "You didn't wear much of anything on the one you went on with me." As if she'd gone on twenty more honeymoons since.

She looked at him coolly. "I don't remember." It was a silly thing to say.

His mouth quirked, but there was no humor in it. "Oh," he said lazily, "I think you do."

Of course she did. They'd spent three idyllic weeks on a tiny Caribbean island hideaway with a private beach. There had been few occasions necessitating anything more than a bikini. Happy days, happy nights. She'd been so in love with him then, this strong, quiet man who'd made the most wonderful love to her. This same man who stood here now—the same voice, the same mouth and hands, the same undeniable male appeal of his strong, lean body. How could she ever forget his lovemaking? And last night—no, early this morning, in bed with him—how she had longed for it then, his love-making, his touch...to feel again the way he'd used to make her feel, that magic sense of rapture.

Suddenly her knees felt weak. She stared blindly at the T-shirt in her hands.

How could she manage the next few days with him alone in this house? How could she talk to him, look at him, watch him move... Oh, God, what was happening to her? Where was her sanity, her common sense?

I can't do this, she thought. *I can't do this*!

CHAPTER FOUR

NICKY was acutely aware of Blake watching her, reading her thoughts. Probably. Maybe. She focused on the label in the T-shirt, concentrating on the fiber content, the washing instructions—anything to divert her thoughts and calm her frazzled nerves. It was impossible. She had to get out of the place as soon as possible. She could not stay here with him in the same house, alone, tormented by unwanted memories and yearnings.

She made a show of folding the T-shirt, her gaze down on her hands. "I want to call my father and tell him to find a way to send me my clothes and my passport," she said, trying to keep her voice steady. "I don't want to stay here any longer than necessary. I don't want to impose."

"We were talking about our honeymoon." He straightened away from the doorjamb and moved toward her.

"And I'm talking about getting out of here," she snapped, automatically looking up at him.

"Are the memories too disturbing?" he asked, meeting her eyes.

"It's all a long time ago." She tried to sound indifferent, but her voice trembled.

He held her gaze. "But not too long to forget, is it?" And it was there, in his voice—pain and yearning mirroring her own.

She clenched her hands, fighting for calmness, terrified to be overwhelmed by emotion. "What are you getting at, Blake? What do you want me to say?"

"I'm not sure. Something to the effect that our marriage was real to you at the time—no matter that it ended, no matter what the reason."

Her stomach churned. "Real, as opposed to what?"

"A fake, a game of pretense." He pushed his hands into his pockets.

Hot tears filled her eyes. "How dare you ask that! How could you even *think* that!" she said huskily, angry at herself for losing her composure.

He shook his head. "I couldn't." He turned away from her, moving toward the door. As he left the room, he glanced at her over his shoulder.

"I came to tell you that if you're thirsty, Ramyah put drinks out for us on the veranda."

He left and she busied herself putting the clothes away, trying to steady her nerves. It was crazy to let herself get so affected by him. She'd have to keep her cool and not let memories get the better of her. Be calm, be in control, she told herself. She grimaced. Such brave words.

Having finished with the clothes she took a deep breath to fortify herself and ventured to the veranda. Blake was sitting in a chair, drinking from a tall glass, reading a book. Not a novel, her glimpse told her, but something about global marketing strategies.

The wide, covered veranda was like an open room, with comfortable furniture, reading lamps and tubs of flowering plants. She poured herself some of the juice from the pitcher on the tray on the table and took a sip. It was deliciously sweet and tangy. Feeling too restless to sit down, she sauntered over to the veranda railing and took in the view.

"It's very dramatic," she said, gesturing at the panorama of mountains and blue sky.

"Yes." It was all he said.

She contemplated the forest-covered hills. "Do people live in the jungle here? I mean, like the Indians in the Amazon?"

"Yes. They're called the *orang asli*, the original people. They're nomadic hunters and gatherers, but there aren't very many left leading the traditional life."

She tried to imagine what it would be like to live in the forest, but couldn't. She leaned her arms on the wooden railing and surveyed the garden below, discovering to her delight a neatly laid-out plot with plants and vines to the left. "They have a vegetable garden!" she said, hearing her voice rise a little with her enthusiasm. "I'm going to have a look."

"You can go down the stairs over there," he suggested, pointing to the far end of the veranda.

She skipped down the creaking steps and followed the path to the vegetable plot, which had been fenced in, probably to keep destructive forest creatures out. She walked between the rows, seeing several kinds of lettuce, hot chili peppers, curly endive, green beans, tomatoes trained on bamboo stakes, and a big patch of strawberries. Strawberries in the tropics? Amazing!

To her surprise she found Blake next to her a few minutes later. "Looks good," he commented, surveying the neat rows.

She sighed longingly. "I'd die for a garden like this. Imagine having all this wonderful, fresh stuff to cook with!" She moved her hand gently through a clump of basil. "This smells so great," she said, moving her face closer. "I love the smell of basil."

He was watching her with an odd expression in his eyes.

She frowned at him. "What? Did I say something wrong?"

"No," he said tersely.

She bent down near the strawberries. "Look, there are a lot of ripe ones. Don't they look beautiful, that bright red amid all that fresh green? A work of art, really. We'd better pick them and have them for dessert."

"Just leave them." There was a sharp edge to his voice and she glanced up, surprised. His eyes were a dull, metal gray, unreadable. She frowned.

"Does it matter if we pick a few?"

"Leave it to the gardener. He doesn't like it if people interfere with his work."

She stared at him. "Don't be ridiculous."

He shrugged, his face stony. "Suit yourself." He marched off, back to the veranda. She watched him, puzzled. What was the matter with him? What had she done to irritate him? It had nothing to do with the strawberries, or the gardener, she was sure. Earlier today in the village market he'd been irritable and impatient as well. This moody, short-tempered man was not the Blake she remembered.

She shrugged off the thought and picked a few berries and ate them slowly, savoring them. There was nothing here to put them in to carry them back to the house, so she might as well enjoy them right here and give Blake a little space.

Back on the veranda, she poured herself another glass of juice. Blake was reading his book again, legs stretched out and crossed at the ankles. A small white scar stood out against the tanned skin of his foot. A childhood injury he'd contracted while trying to rescue a frog out of the cruel hands of a neighborhood boy. Chasing the bigger boy, Blake, barefoot, had fallen and cut himself on a piece of glass. Lots of blood. The other boy had fled in fear, throwing down the frog.

Her heart contracted. Blake's mother had told her the story, and the image of Blake as a little boy saving a frog was touching. She moved her gaze to a wooden tub of coral impatiens blooming enthusiastically a few feet away. She had to stop thinking about him, remembering things. The best way to do that was not to be in his presence.

She put the glass on the table. "I'd like to call my fath—" She stopped herself, feeling her heart sink. "I don't suppose there's a telephone all the way up here?"

He put his book down. "There's a cellular one. It works on radio waves. It's in the office." He pushed himself to his feet. "Come on, I'll show you how to use it."

The office was a huge room with one wall entirely taken up with windows. Underneath them, wide planks of polished wood resting on filing cabinets functioned as desk space. Another wall was covered with maps and photographs of plants. The two remaining walls were taken up with bamboo shelving full of books, magazines and office materials.

A muffled curse made her turn around. "What's the matter?"

Blake was scowling down at a small black box on the table. "The receiver is gone. Let me check with Ramyah." He charged out of the room.

She entertained herself by studying the maps and photographs on the wall. The maps appeared to be of the surrounding forest, indicating locations where various plant species had been found. The photos were beautiful, technically as well as artistically, and she was quite content studying them.

Blake didn't look any happier when he returned a while later, the missing receiver in his hand—in pieces.

"For what it's worth," he said flatly, "the mystery of why Ramyah was so nervous, is solved." He slid the jumble of wires and metal pieces onto the table next to the base.

"How did that happen?" Nicky asked, surveying the mess. "This doesn't happen just by dropping it!"

"No. This happens when a curious seven-year-old decides to take it apart to see what's inside and what makes it work."

Nicky groaned. "Oh, no. Whose kid? Hers?"

He nodded. "She took him to work with her last Saturday and you can guess the rest." He grimaced. "She was afraid she'd be fired."

Nicky sighed. "No wonder she was a nervous wreck. What did you tell her?"

"That it was an accident and she's not getting fired, of course, and that the O'Connors will arrange for another phone when they get back." He ran his hand through his hair. "Damn," he muttered. "I don't understand the woman."

"You don't understand what?" Nicky asked, surprised. "You mean that she lost track of the kid so he could wreak his havoc with this thing?"

He waved his hand impatiently. "No, of course not."

"Then what?"

"Think of this," he said. "Ramyah has been with the O'Connors for twelve years. She keeps this place running like clockwork, no matter how many students or other people invade the place. She's worth her weight in gold. They'd be lost without her, and they know it." He gave an exasperated sigh. "And here she is, terrified she'll be fired over a damn phone! You should have seen her a minute ago. She was shaking like a leaf when she brought me the stuff. She'd been praying all night for forgiveness."

Nicky felt a wave a pity. "I feel sorry for her."

"But why does she feel this way, for heaven's sake? Why doesn't she know her own worth?"

Nicky shrugged helplessly. "I have no idea. Maybe it's culture, or something. Or maybe nobody ever actually *told* her she was worth her weight in gold."

He frowned impatiently. "I can't understand why she wouldn't know."

"How are you supposed to know what other people think if they don't tell you? Are you supposed to read their minds?"

He gave an exasperated sigh. "Oh, for God's sake, Nicky, I'm not going to argue about this." He swept up the bits and pieces of the receiver and dumped them unceremoniously into the wastepaper basket. "I don't think we'll need this anymore."

"So now we have no phone," Nicky stated unnecessarily.

"Right. Cut off from the civilized world we are," he said indifferently. "I, for one, don't care. A little peace and quiet won't hurt me at all."

Irritation swelled inside her. "That's all good and well, but in the meantime I'm sitting here not knowing what's going on with my father!"

He nodded, his expression softening. "Don't worry about your father, Nicky. He's a smart man."

"That's easy for you to say!" She clenched her hands, feeling suddenly close to tears. "I can't believe this is happening to me! I hate not knowing what to do, to just...sit here!"

"It's the best you can do for now."

"Well, it isn't good enough!"

His jaw tensed. "Complaining isn't going to get you anywhere. You might want to consider what would have happened if I hadn't been able to get to you in time. You might have found yourself in a place much less agreeable than this one."

The thought alone cooled her considerably. He was right. Of course he was right. She dragged in a calming breath of air. "I'm sorry," she said, trying to infuse her voice with a little mature dignity. "My nerves were getting the better of me. I'll work on them." She was going to stay in control of her emotions if it killed her. She wasn't going to complain.

She caught the silver glint deep in his eyes, but had no idea how to interpret it. She didn't know his thoughts. Had she ever really known his thoughts?

She turned and went back into the living room which also had a wall of shelving containing books and magazines in both French and English.

To her delight she found a wonderful collection of books on native foods, herbal medicines, and a cookbook on aphrodisiacs and love potions. She took them to her room and read through them, enjoying the strange tales and myths. There was an article in there somewhere. She'd have to give it some thought.

Ramyah served them a delicious meal that night, flavorful, spicy food which Nicky enjoyed thoroughly.

"Does Ramyah live in the village?" she asked Blake, trying for some conversation. He had said little since the start of the meal.

He nodded. "Yes, but during the week she and Ali stay in the servants' quarters at the back of the house. They go home on Thursday night and come back Saturday afternoon."

Nicky went on talking, about her writing, about the success of her book, about the book she was writing now. After a while it was clear that she was doing most of the talking and annoyance began to creep through her.

"Listen," she said, "I'm trying to be pleasant and keep up my part of the conversation, but a little feedback would be appreciated."

"I'm sorry, but I don't feel like talking." He scraped back his chair. "I've work to do, excuse me."

She stood up, too, her heart suddenly pounding. What was the matter with this man? She did not recognize him. She faced him squarely.

"I'm sorry if you don't find my company stimulating, but I don't believe it's necessary for you to be rude about it."

He stood still, his gaze meeting hers for a moment. Dark shadows, hesitation. "It was not my intention to offend you," he stated evenly. "I apologize." No expression on his face.

"You didn't used to be so irritable," she stated. "What is it I'm doing that ticks you off every time?"

"Nothing," he said tersely.

She stared at him. "Nothing I do. Maybe it's just my presence? You don't want me here. You don't even want to talk to me."

"I offered my apologies."

"And that's supposed to make me feel better? Well, I'm not here because I want to be here! I'm here because *you* brought me here!"

"I'm supremely aware of that." He closed his eyes briefly. "I am also supremely aware of you."

Her heart lurched. "Aware of me?"

"Yes." His voice was tight. "You used to be my wife. I watch you enjoy the market, see your face as you look at the strawberries in the garden, I hear you talk about your work, and all I can think of is how you're still that same woman who was my wife. And that now you're not."

Her throat constricted. She couldn't think of a thing to say.

He sighed, the shuttered look back in his eyes. "Nicky, I'm sorry. This isn't easy for either of us. We'll just have to manage somehow."

"I was trying to manage," she said miserably.

He raked his hands through his hair. "Yes, you're right. I'm sorry."

She bit her lip. "It's all right. Forget it."

He went to his office and she was relieved to see him leave. Ramyah brought her coffee and she took it to the veranda, where several mosquito coils were already burning, the thin spirals of smoke trailing up into the air.

Noises came from the forest beyond the garden—a whoop-whooping Ramyah had told her came from monkeys, odd animal cries, shrieks, hoots and whistles, the drone and buzzing of millions of insects.

She thought of Blake in his office, escaping from her. How odd to be with him in the same house, to eat her meals with him. She felt her throat close. Once she'd thought they'd be together always. She'd been so sure, so confident. She remembered the night she'd told her parents she and Blake were getting married, the memory of the conversation clear as if it had taken place only yesterday.

Her parents had liked Blake, but had been concerned about her marrying so young, before even finishing her college education. And so soon after meeting him.

"We've got it all figured out!" she'd told them. "Don't worry about it."

Her father's smile had been amused. "All figured out?" he'd asked, humor in his voice. "Princess, when it comes to marriage you never have it all figured out. Situations change, you make adjustments. You'll mature and change. He'll change. You have to *keep* figuring it out."

"Oh, Dad, I know that!" She'd been impatient, annoyed a little. Her father always knew everything so well, always treated her as if she were just a little girl. "But we can't just jump in without talking about it and hope we'll just manage without agreeing on a few things!"

Her mother nodded. "Of course, you're right. So what did you agree on?"

"We're going to leave each other free." She'd stopped there, on purpose, to get a little rise out of her parents. The devil made her do it.

Her mother looked worried. "*Free*? Free to do what?"

Nicky laughed. "Free to follow our own careers, free to make our own decisions. We're not going to make silly demands on each other and tell each other what to do."

"I see," her father said carefully.

"Which means, basically," she went on, taking a deep breath, "that Blake is going to do his traveling and I'm not going to whine and moan about his being gone so much. I have my own career to think about, after all. I'm going to finish college. I'm going to keep writing and when I have my degree I'll be able to travel with him on some of his assignments." Excitement rose inside her. "I can't wait to go with him. It'll be so great!"

"Blake will be gone weeks at a time," her mother said with a worried expression. "Are you sure you can handle that?"

"Yes, I am, Mom. I'm an independent person and I shouldn't depend on him to fill every moment of my life with meaning and happiness. I have that responsibility myself." It sounded so mature, she was proud of herself. She grinned. "But when he comes home we'll be together and it will be special. We'll appreciate each other more. We won't get into a rut so easily."

Her mother glanced over at her father. "They've done some thinking about it."

Her father nodded. "I've known Blake for years and I like him very much, you know that. He's a sensible, responsible man and we'll just have to have faith that the two of you will make it work. All we really want is for you to be happy."

"Oh, I'll be happy. I know I will!"

In bed that night, she had heard again her father's voice. *He's a sensible, responsible man.* She'd grinned up at the ceiling. How hopelessly dull that sounded! To her, Blake was exciting, intriguing and utterly sexy. He was cosmopolitan and knew his way around the world. Blake was a real man, sure of himself and his convictions. He did not throw temper tantrums, he did not force his opinion on other people. She'd never seen him angry—annoyed, yes, but not really angry. He was so marvelously even-tempered.

He was, in many ways, very different than she. For one thing, she did get angry, and passionate, too, about things that she cared about. Sometimes that made him laugh. He thought she was amusing for caring so much, for spending so much energy on enjoying things he'd never even thought about. He laughed when she got excited about the daffodils coming up in spring, or the growing of her small pots of herbs in her windowsill, or about a wonderful new recipe she'd found. He loved her and she loved him. They enjoyed each other, made each other happy.

A frightening shriek from the forest pulled her back to the present. Not all was peaceful in the jungle. Some creature out there was not having a good time.

She sighed. At twenty-one she'd been so naive. It hurt to think about it now, to remember the feelings, the words she had said. To know how truly she had meant them, how very much she had been in love with Blake. She'd been so confident that they would make their marriage work.

After the divorce she'd felt dead inside for a long time—years, in fact. Until Jim had come onto the scene. Jim was a hard-nosed reporter on the job and a softy in private. He knew how to say the right words at the right time. He'd thawed out her reserve and made her feel again—a little, anyway. But it had not been enough to try again, to make a commitment. They'd seen each other for over a year, until it was clear to her that it would not be fair to him to keep the relationship going, even though it was nice and comfortable, even though she liked and respected him very much.

She'd liked him very much, but she hadn't loved him, at least not in the right way. Something was missing. He had never touched the deepest core of her—maybe because she hadn't allowed him to, she wasn't sure.

She stirred restlessly. She needed something to do, something to occupy her mind. She could not spend the next few days brooding over the failures in her life. It was not productive. It was over and done with.

She came to her feet as Blake stepped out onto the veranda. She hadn't heard him approach and it took her by surprise. "I thought you were working," she said.

"My mind's not on it." He frowned. "You don't have to leave."

"I was going to my room. Besides, I know you'd rather be alone."

She saw him tense. "Oh, for God's sake," he said irritably. "Let's not play games. We're not going to be able to avoid each other, so let's not even try, all right?"

"I wasn't trying to avoid you," she said, feeling anger rise at his tone. "I was just getting up to go to my room and try to do some writing. That's all."

He shrugged, his jaw a hard line. "Suit yourself."

She moved past him into the house and went to her room. She found paper and pens in the desk, probably left there by a student or guest. Today had offered quite a crop of writing topics, and it didn't matter where she started. She needed to get the stuff on paper and work out what to do with it later. She needed to get her mind off Blake.

If ever you're the victim of a cosmic joke and find yourself cruising through the Malaysian tea plantations with your ex-husband, try to divert your mind from this unsavory situation by contemplating the mysteries of tea.

Before you read the rest of this article, brew yourself a proper pot of tea. No bags in ugly mugs, please! You will need a glass cup, or if this is not available, a white cup—it may have flowers on the outside, but not on the inside.

Fill the cup. Now hold it in the sunlight, or if not available, lamplight. Look at the color, truly savor the rich, burnished red. Isn't it wonderful? It's like a jewel in the light. I get excited about that stuff. I just can't help myself.

She reread it, groaned and dropped her head on the desk. She was exhausted and her head felt very heavy. After a few minutes she struggled upright, tore up her writing and went to bed.

Mist-shrouded mountains greeted her as she peered sleepily out the window the next morning. The air was cool and damp. She pulled on a pair of jeans, rolling up the legs and tightening the waist with a belt. They were at least a size too big, but loose was the fashion. It was cool enough to wear socks and sneakers, which she found. The shoes were a size too big, as well, but tightening the laces would keep them on her feet. She pulled a sweatshirt on over a T-shirt, then went in search of breakfast.

Blake was not in evidence and she assumed he was working in the office. She had breakfast alone and then tried to talk to Ramyah, which was a bit of a struggle. Nicky knew ten words of Malay, and Ramyah, twenty of English.

The kitchen was simple, but functional, and the pantry was large and impressive, storing good supplies of non-perishables, many of gourmet standard. No one was living a deprived life in this house.

She was about to go for a stroll in the garden when Blake entered the kitchen, a coffee cup in his hand.

"Good morning," he said, looking her up and down, his mouth curling with amusement. "You look charming."

She glared at him. "It's not my fault that these clothes are too big for me. And if you don't like it, don't look at me!"

His eyebrows shot up. "Ouch. You are snappish this morning. Where's your sense of humor?"

She gritted her teeth. "I left it behind along with my own clothes and purse and the rest of my life when you abducted me."

"I did not abduct you. I rescued you," he corrected her.

She waved her hand as if the distinction was of no consequence. "Whatever. But that doesn't mean I'm supposed to *like* being here with you."

"No one's asking you to," he said coolly. "It wasn't exactly my idea of fun, either." He picked up the coffeepot and filled his cup.

"If you don't want me here, you could have figured out something else," she said hotly.

"I promised your father I'd take care of you, and I will." His tone was calm and determined.

"Take care of me?"

"Keep you safe."

"How cozy," she said nastily. She wasn't being fair, she knew, yet she seemed unable to contain herself. "Well, you'll just have to tolerate my presence, unsavory as it may be to you, and no matter how uncharming I look in these clothes!"

"I wasn't complaining." His mouth curved faintly. "Somehow, dear Nicky, you manage to look sexy no matter what you wear."

She glared at him. "I have absolutely no desire to look sexy, feel sexy, or be sexy, rest assured."

"That's a relief," he said dryly. "It might complicate matters."

"I've no intention of complicating matters. I just want to keep things simple."

He nodded. "You and I in the same house, in different beds. Very simple."

"Exactly."

He gave her a long look. "Don't fool yourself, Nicky," he said quietly. "It won't be easy. It's already not easy."

There was an awkward silence, the truth of his words like a living presence between them. She searched desperately for something to say, something light or funny, or even something sarcastic—anything to break the uneasiness, but her mind produced nothing.

"Well," he said slowly, breaking the silence. "I'd better get back to work." He moved to the door. "See you later."

She released a long, slow breath. Then, resolutely, she put his words out of her mind and went outside and began to explore the garden. Chickens ran loose around and under the house. She discovered a large tank which she assumed held gasoline to fuel the generator, and a rugged pickup truck that looked like it had done hard labor.

At the end of the garden, she found a narrow trail leading into the forest. Standing in the bright sunlight she considered the possibility of a brief foray down the green, shadowy trail, contemplating the dangers. Obviously, this trail was one she'd seen on the maps in the office, used by the O'Connors and the students.

Glancing down she examined her jeans and sneakers. Surely they'd do. She'd go for a short while only, and go straight and come back straight.

It was getting warmer and she pulled off the sweatshirt and tossed it on the grass. She'd get it on her way back. Ten yards down the path and she felt as if she'd been swallowed by an ancient, primordial world, vibrating with secret life. Glancing over her shoulder she could no longer see the sunny garden with its riot of flowering bushes. She continued, looking carefully where she was setting her feet. The path was wet and slippery from rain that must have fallen during the night.

Sunlight filtered thinly through the canopy of leaves above, sparking here and there on the wet, dripping foliage. Huge ferns clung to tree trunks, mosses drooped down from branches and vines. Unseen birds chattered in the verdant greenery and everywhere was the humming and buzzing of insects.

It was like magic. She felt awed by it all.

Just as she decided to turn back, she heard the rushing of water. Going on a few more steps, she noticed a fast-running stream babbling over rocks and stones, the water crystal clear. Bending down she put her hand in it to feel it. It was icy cold.

She found a flat rock and sat down and watched a cloud of brightly colored butterflies dancing in the dappled sunlight. How wonderful it would be to have someone to share this with. The thought brought back memories of camping trips and hikes with Blake in the Blue Ridge Mountains, of sitting by idyllic streams by day and intimate fires at night. Impatiently she pushed the images away and came to her feet again. It was time to go back.

She'd barely straightened up when she noticed the snake coiled comfortably on a sunny rock, a mere four feet away from her. Her heart leapt in her throat. Inching away carefully, she made her retreat, her eyes on the motionless reptile. It never stirred, uninterested in her presence.

Once at a safe distance, she let out a long sigh of relief and grinned at herself. She'd seen snakes before and had learned to accept them as a reality of life, but she'd never learned to be fond of them.

Her heart rate slowed to normal as she moved on down the trail. She was almost back to the house when she heard her name. Blake, calling her. She saw him a moment later, coming toward her around a bend in the trail, wearing khaki shorts and a black T-shirt. She couldn't help but feel the little leap in her chest at seeing the familiar shape of him, the long, muscular legs striding so purposefully toward her, the movements of his lean body, all male and sexy amid the verdant greenery of the jungle. She swallowed hard, pushing the thoughts out of her head.

"I'm here," she said. "I just went for a walk. It's so beautiful here!" She was about to elaborate about all the wonderful things she had seen, when her enthusiasm was abruptly squashed by the glowering expression on his face.

"What the hell do you think you're doing disappearing like this!"

She stared at him. "I was taking a walk. I was only gone for half an hour or so."

"You should have told somebody!" Anger flashed in his eyes. "This is not a city park, for God's sake! Look around you!" He made a sweeping gesture with his arm, as if to demonstrate. "This is the *rain forest*! It's what they used to call the *jungle*!"

She stiffened. "Thank you for that information. I hadn't noticed," she said sarcastically.

His jaw worked. His eyes bored into hers. "Do you have any idea how dangerous it is out here?"

She crossed her arms in front of her chest as she thought of the snake. "I think I have some idea, yes."

"For future reference, if you want to go on a stroll, tell someone and don't ever set a single footstep off the path or you may never find it again."

"I'll remember that," she said frigidly. "And for future reference, will you remember not to speak to me as if I'm a dim-witted child?"

"Then don't act like one!"

He walked off, then turned abruptly and waited for her to catch up.

"Do you play golf?" he asked.

She stared at him with open mouth. "What?" she asked.

"Golf," he repeated impatiently. "Do you play golf?"

She laughed, she couldn't help it. One moment he was berating her about taking a walk in the jungle and the next he was inquiring if she played golf.

He shoved his hands into his pockets. "What's so funny? It's a simple question, isn't it?"

She nodded. "Yes. And no, I don't play golf. You know I don't."

He shrugged and began walking again. "A lot can change in four years."

So it could, but not that particular situation. "Why do you ask?" She had trouble keeping up with his long strides.

"I'm going down to Paradise Mountain, the resort we passed by on the way over here. I need to make some phone calls and I thought I'd take in a round of golf and have dinner there with some friends. Would you like to come?"

She certainly would love to have a phone to use and to be someplace where there were other people besides Blake.

"I'd love to. I'd like to call my father."

"Fine. There's a swimming pool, and a small shop where you can buy a suit."

They left right after lunch, bumping along the unpaved track for about twenty minutes before coming to the little village where the paved road began. It wound back down the mountains, through tea plantations and market gardens and back up again toward the resort. It took another half hour before they entered the gates of Paradise Mountain.

Blake parked the car in a shady lot near the main building, a rustic construction of stone and wood. "I don't mean to worry you more than necessary," he said, looking at her, "but when you call your father, be careful of what you say. I don't want this to sound like something out of a bad movie, but for all I know his phones may be tapped. Don't tell him where you are. He already knows. I mentioned I'd be here to write my report when I spoke to him at the party. Also, don't talk about that business scam he's dealing with. And don't ask for your passport, either. Better safe than sorry."

She stared at him. "I don't believe this," she said on a sigh. "How am I going to get my purse and my passport!"

"I'll figure something out."

"Like what?"

He made an impatient gesture. "For the time being it's not very important. Just tell your father that you're all right. He has enough on his mind right now."

She closed her eyes briefly and sighed. "All right, I'll be careful. What *do* I talk to him about?"

He shrugged. "Tell him you're at a party and having a great time."

She looked at him, saw a flicker of humor in his eyes. "You've got to be kidding," she said on a low note.

He took the key out of the ignition and put it in his pocket. "Alternatively, you can tell him you're having a terrible time, but that might worry him." He opened the door and leapt out of the car.

Inside the building, he took her to the manager's office, where she was introduced to a sophisticated Malay man who greeted them with a smile. He spoke English fluently, and it was obvious he knew Blake from several previous visits. He was a friend of the O'Connors who came to the resort regularly to play golf and tennis and to visit with friends who lived in the area.

They were offered the use of a room where they could change clothes and make their phone calls. Blake suggested she go ahead and call her father, after which he would show her the resort shop and the pool.

Her call took no time at all; her father was not in his office. The secretary informed her that he was at an important meeting at the Ministry of Industry and Commerce and was not expected back in the office that afternoon. She put the phone down, feeling deflated and worried.

"Try again later," Blake suggested. "I'll show you around first." He pulled out his wallet and fished out a credit card. "Buy what you need," he told her, handing her the piece of gold plastic.

She had no choice but to accept it, but it made her cringe. It made her feel like a bothersome child sent out of the way. "I'll pay you back," she said tightly.

"I'm sure you will." The corner of his mouth twitched and it was that little smile that sparked something in her.

"Don't smirk at me!" she snapped.

The twitch turned into a half grin. "Wasn't aware I was smirking," he said casually.

"Are you enjoying this?"

"Enjoying what? Lending you some money? What's the big deal?"

"You enjoy seeing me so helpless and dependent on your good graces!" She hated this. To be dependent on her own ex-husband, of all people, was almost intolerable.

"I wouldn't have a nervous breakdown about it if I were you," he said with maddening calm. "Now, come this way, and I'll show you where the pool is."

He was insufferable! She couldn't stand him! It took an effort to keep her cool. Nervous breakdown, my foot, she said silently. I'll show you!

They followed flower-fringed walking paths until the crystal blue water of the pool appeared in front of them. It was large, shaped irregularly and surrounded by lounges in sunny spots and small tables in the shade. Planters full of flowers offered an abundance of cheerful color. An open-air coffee shop on one end dispensed drinks and snacks. Spending a few hours here would be no hardship.

They went back to the main building, which contained a restaurant as well as the sports shop whose window displayed an artfully arranged collection of fashionable swim and sports wear.

"I'll go make my phone calls and head for the golf course," Blake announced. "Let's say we'll meet at six at the restaurant terrace for sundowners. All right?"

She nodded. "Fine, I'll see you there." She moved inside the store, narrowly passing a young woman on her way out. Of Indian descent, she had shiny black hair and large brown eyes. Even the brief glimpse that Nicky caught of her was enough to see she was strikingly beautiful.

Nicky glanced around the store to orient herself.

"Blake!" she heard the woman say behind her back. Automatically, Nicky turned around to see her hugging a smiling Blake.

"Hello, Ghita," he returned cheerfully.

"Lisette told me you were coming. I was hoping you'd get in touch." She had a nice voice and a sexy accent.

She was dressed in a simple white dress modestly accenting perfect shapes and curves. "You know," she went on, "I'm not—"

Nicky couldn't hear the rest. She watched the two moving away and out of sight. She realized she was staring into empty space, not moving, her mouth dry as dust. She swallowed hard and turned back again to start her exploration of the store.

The shop was well-stocked with all the usual items found in resort stores—swimwear and casual clothes, sports gear, sunglasses and toiletry articles. Not surprisingly, the prices were astronomical. Well, no matter. She had a magic piece of plastic, gold and shiny. She might as well use it.

An hour later she had what she wanted—a bikini, a wrap to cover up, sunscreen, sunglasses, moisturizer and some makeup. She'd also bought a long cotton dress made of traditional Malay *batek* fabric with an exotic design in brown, white and indigo blue. She'd wear that to the restaurant tonight.

Instead of going back to the room, where she might run into Blake, and God forbid, the woman named Ghita, she changed in the shower room near the pool. She ordered a glass of juice from the coffee shop and settled herself on a lounge. Having slathered sunscreen all over herself like a responsible person, she closed her eyes and sighed.

Ah, bliss.

But not for long. Voices. Laughter. People were settling at a table nearby. Words and phrases reached her ears. Something about a dinner party, a tennis match. Two girls, by the sound of it, and she recognized one of the voices.

Nicky turned her face and peered through her lashes. Ghita, as she had suspected. She was sitting at a small table nearby, in the company of another woman, a tall blonde. Both of them looked young, in their early twenties. Both of them wore bikinis and were sipping drinks. Ghita leaned forward a little, pushing her drink aside.

"Guess who I ran into a few moments ago?" she asked.

CHAPTER FIVE

GHITA'S voice was breathless with excitement and Nicky stiffened. She knew the answer to that question.

"Who?" asked the skinny blonde.

"Blake. Blake Chandler. Remember I introduced him to you...oh, I think it was almost a year ago. He's American, tall and handsome and—"

"How could I forget?" said the blonde, laughing. "You wouldn't stop talking about him. He's the most wonderful, sexy, considerate, dynamic, intelligent man who ever walked the face of the earth. An absolute paragon of virtue and virility. No sins, no faults."

"Go ahead and laugh, but it's true. He..."

Nicky was beginning to feel very hot. Well, she was sitting in the sun. She reached for her passion fruit juice and sipped it. She didn't want to hear more, but it was impossible to block out the sound of the voices. They were discussing the fact that Blake was not married, that his wife had divorced him some years ago.

"Makes you wonder what happened," commented the blonde, her voice dry. "Why would any woman voluntarily let go of such a perfect man?"

"A not-so-bright one." There was a harsh note in Ghita's sexy voice.

Nicky felt like jumping up and confronting them, telling them they didn't know what they were talking about, that they had no idea what went on behind closed doors in other people's lives. That it was extremely unintelligent to judge when they knew nothing of the facts.

She lay immobilized on the lounge, her heart thumping wildly, trying to tell herself that this was ridiculous, really. Hilarious, actually. No reason for her to get all frazzled because of these naive college girls—hardly women, really. Perhaps she should make a little comedy out of the situation. Come to her feet, smile nicely, say she had overheard them and wouldn't mind letting them in on a few of the juicy details about Mr. Perfect's failed marriage. That once she had been extremely close to Mr. Perfect and his stupid ex-wife and that she had all manner of confidential information and intimate details.

Her imagination and creativity failed her miserably. No matter how she fiddled with various versions of the scenario, she couldn't make it funny.

There was nothing funny about being away from home and calling your husband in the middle of the night and not finding him in bed. And it didn't get any funnier when you called him the next night and the night after that, and he was never there. Her teeth hurt. She was clenching them too hard.

"He's never getting married again," she heard Ghita say. "He told me so. God knows what she must have done to him."

Nicky went rigid. Her breathing was shallow. Rage tasted bitter in her mouth. How dare she! What did she think she had done to him?

"A good woman should be able to change his mind," stated the blonde. "How good are you, Ghita?"

Laughter. Nicky clenched her hands into fists. She couldn't stand this. She took off the sunglasses, got up from the lounge and dove into the pool. She didn't want to hear another word.

God knows what she must have done to him. Even under the water the echoes of Ghita's voice followed her.

She swam back and forth across the deep end of the pool, back and forth as if in training for the Olympics.

Finally, exhausted, she hauled herself out of the water and sat on the edge of the pool and checked out the surroundings. The women were still there. Well, she'd just get her stuff and move to a lounge on the other side of the pool. She had no appetite for any more of their conversation.

She made her move, ordered another drink and picked up the book she'd brought and began to read. A story about an art treasure hunt in the rocky interior of Iceland.

What she liked about Veigar, she read, *was his calm, quiet self-possession. He was the most intelligent, sexy man she had ever met. He spoke little. She was intrigued by those calm gray eyes, by what lay hidden in the silence.*

Nicky groaned and flung the book onto the grass. If ever she gathered enough courage to get married again, it had better be someone with a stormy nature who expressed every little thought that entered his mind. A lyrical Italian, or a passionate Greek.

She groaned again. Forget it. She was never, never getting married again.

At the end of an endless afternoon, she went back to the room, bracing herself to find Blake there getting ready for the evening.

The room was empty and she expelled a sigh of relief. The bathroom showed signs of use—steam and the scent of soap and shampoo. Good, he'd been here and had left; she had the place to herself.

At six o'clock sharp she arrived at the restaurant terrace and found Blake sitting at a table with the lovely Ghita. She clenched her jaws together. Oh, damn. That's just what she needed—she and Ghita being introduced to each other. *Ghita, this is Nicky Arnell, my ex-wife.* She'd smile at Ghita, and say, *You know, the one you were discussing this afternoon, the not-so-bright one.*

*You were wondering what she might have done to poor,
perfect Blake.*

Oh, stop it, she told herself. She stretched her spine,
produced a brilliant smile and sashayed over to the small
table, the soft cotton of her *batek* dress moving smoothly
around her ankles.

"Hi," she said cheerfully.

They looked up. Blake came to his feet and held out
a chair for her, making introductions as he did so, sup-
plying only names and no relationships. Cool, reserved
Blake. She should have known that's what he'd do.

"How was your afternoon?" he asked politely, and
she told him it had been wonderfully relaxing, which of
course was the lie of the century.

When the waiter appeared she asked for a Midnight
Moon Dance, one of the exotic mixed drinks on the menu
featuring an abundance of alcohol. She sensed more than
noticed Blake's surprise. She'd never used to drink anything stronger than wine, and she still didn't often. Right
now wine seemed too tame a drink for the mood she
was in.

Her drink arrived only moments later, complete with
a paper parasol and pineapple butterfly. Blake rose to
his feet and asked if they could possibly do without his
presence for a few minutes; he needed to make a phone
call. Ghita smiled sweetly and said they could do without
him.

Of course they could. They could chat and get to know
each other. Do some female bonding. Nicky took the
pineapple from the rim of the glass and chewed it. Oh,
God, what was the matter with her? Why was she feeling
so bitchy? It was not her nature to feel so negative and
ungracious. This woman—this girl—was obviously in
love with Blake and there was no reason why she
shouldn't be. There was no reason why it should bother

her, the ex-wife. She took a generous swallow of her drink.

Blake departed and Nicky was aware that Ghita scrutinized her with ill-concealed curiosity. Nicky offered her a smile. "This is a beautiful place," she said for something to say.

Ghita moistened her lips. "Yes."

"Are you on vacation here?" Nicky asked, having no great hopes for a meaningful discussion.

"No. I live not far from here. My father owns the place."

Nicky digested this information, but wasn't sure if it was useful. She nodded.

The conversation struggled on for a few more minutes.

"Where did you meet Blake?" Ghita asked, curiosity obviously getting the better of her.

"At a cocktail party in KL," Nicky answered, a little devil stirring inside her. "Three days ago."

There was silence for a moment. Nicky smiled at Ghita. "He invited me to come with him to the mountains while he wrote his report. It's beautiful here. I love it."

Ghita's eyes were wide with amazement. "You met him at a cocktail party three days ago and he invited you to come with him?" she echoed.

Nicky nodded solemnly. "It all happened rather quickly, I know. But it seemed like we'd known each other forever. You know how that feels sometimes when you meet someone?"

Ghita nodded slowly, but her expression lacked conviction. Something else flickered in the dark eyes—anger? Suspicion? Nicky wasn't sure.

"Is something wrong?"

"No, I mean, it's not the sort of thing you'd expect him to do. He's . . . not like that."

"I see," said Nicky, knowing it was true. She sipped her drink.

Ghita looked uncomfortable, as if she knew she had to do something, but wasn't sure what.

"You may feel you've known him forever," she began at last, challenge in her voice, "but I've known him a lot longer than three days, and . . . and I think I'm doing you a service by warning you not to expect too much from him."

Nicky felt herself tense. Who did this woman think she was? Claiming territory, was she?

"Thank you for warning me," she said coolly.

Ghita's hands tightened around her glass. She bit her lip. "He was married once, you know," she said, sounding like a rebellious child telling a secret. "Did he tell you that?" There was challenge in her eyes, her voice.

"No," said Nicky truthfully. "He didn't tell me that."

Triumph glittered in Ghita's dark eyes. Her face spoke volumes. *I know more than you do.*

"You can't really know a person in three days," Ghita went on, trying to sound confident, "and it might save you a lot of grief if you didn't get your hopes up."

Nicky allowed a significant silence. There were a couple of ways to play this, but she opted for the easy way out. She managed a bland smile. "Thank you for your concern, but don't worry. I don't want him."

Ghita's mouth began to drop open, but she caught herself. "You don't want him?" she repeated. Clearly, she found the idea hard to grasp.

Nicky shook her head. "No, this is just a . . . eh . . . temporary situation." She finished the last of her drink. "Oh, here he comes now."

She watched Blake approach, taking in the broad shoulders, the confident way he held his head, felt her heart stumbling. He maneuvered around the tables with athletic ease and her stomach tightened. His body exuded a powerful grace and unselfconscious male sexuality and her female senses were hopelessly aware of it.

Reaching the table, he sat down in his chair again and leaned back in it lazily. "Sorry to desert you two," he commented, picking up his glass.

"No problem," said Nicky. "We've become acquainted." She smiled, feeling the little devil stir again. "I told Ghita we met in KL a few days ago and that you invited me to stay with you at the O'Connors' house."

He gave her a searching look. "I see." He offered no further comment, but asked if they were interested in another drink.

"I'd love another Moon Dance, or whatever it was, please," she answered, "and if you would excuse me, I have a phone call to make, as well."

In the room she dialed her father's house. No answer. Not even the housekeeper or one of the other servants picked up the phone. Her chest felt heavy. Where was her father? Maybe he'd gone out for drinks, or dinner. It was still early, surely there was nothing to worry about.

She went back to the table and sat down.

"Any luck?" asked Blake.

She shook her head and picked up her glass. Her hands shook. Blake's eyes narrowed slightly as he observed her. Then he took the glass from her hand and put it down. He glanced at Ghita. "Please, excuse us."

Taking Nicky's hand he came to his feet, drawing her up out of the chair at the same time. "Come with me."

Still holding her hand, he led her down the steps into the shadowed garden, away from the restaurant terrace.

"What's wrong?" he asked.

"He isn't there." Her voice trembled. "He was at the Ministry of Trade and Commerce this afternoon his secretary said, but I'd hoped he'd be home by now." Her chest felt tight.

"He's probably out to dinner. It's only six-thirty."

"I know. I just can't help worrying. I'm scared something might happen to him." She closed her eyes and let out a shaky sigh, feeling at the same time his arms coming around her, drawing her against him.

For a moment she held her breath, standing perfectly still in his embrace, her cheek against his shoulder.

"Why are you doing this?" she whispered then, not drawing away. Leaning into him instead, savoring the comfort.

"I didn't think about it. It just comes naturally, I guess." Lightness in his voice.

She needed lightness, humor. "You always were a good hugger," she said, her voice quivering.

"You always seemed to fit so nicely."

Madness. She fought the yearning flooding through her. This was just a hug for comfort, a caring gesture. After all, Blake was a good guy, a rescuer of terrorized frogs and maidens in distress, a giver of comforting hugs.

It took all her strength to draw out of his embrace. Her body objected, her heart objected. Her mind won. She gave him a shaky smile. "We should get back to the table. Ghita is going to wonder what happened to us."

"Ghita is a big girl. She'll find someone to talk to."

Which she had. Several other people had joined their table and a waiter was taking orders for their dinner.

Mercifully, dinner and the animated conversation at the table distracted her from her preoccupation. The night air was cool and fragrant, and eating the delicious food on the outside terrace was a treat.

The main course finished, Nicky excused herself to make one more attempt at calling her father. The phone rang three times, then her father's voice sounded in her ear.

Her body slumped with relief. "Dad! It's me. I've been trying and trying all day to get hold of you. Are you all right?"

"Of course I'm all right. I've been trying to reach you, too, but it seems your phone is out."

"A little kid took it apart. I'm calling from...a restaurant."

"I hope this little side trip isn't inconveniencing you too much. Are you getting any work done?"

"I'm trying. It's a great place to work. Very good for the creative spirit." If only Blake wouldn't be there. He was disturbing her creative spirit.

"Good, I'm glad." Hesitation in his voice. "I know this is an awkward situation for you, Nicky, but I saw no other solution."

"I know, Dad. I'm all right." What else could she say? I'm having a nervous breakdown? Staying under the same roof with my ex-husband is intolerable? Her father didn't want to have to worry about her. She didn't want him to.

So many questions she didn't dare ask on the phone, so many worries. What if someone overheard them? What if these jokers from Hong Kong were still after her? She was beginning to feel paranoid, but then it might be considered an intelligent reaction to being pursued. She wanted to ask him about her handbag, her passport, tell him she wanted to get out of the country, but knew it wouldn't be wise to mention anything of the sort.

"So how are you faring without me?" she asked, hoping he'd give her some clue.

"I'm doing fine and I have everything under control. You just enjoy your vacation."

I'd rather come back, she wanted to say. I'd rather you sent me my papers and passport so I can get out of the country. She couldn't think of a way to ask.

"How's that cold you have?" she asked, feeling silly trying to talk in code. Her father never had colds. "Is it getting better?"

"It's getting a little better," he said, not missing a beat. "But I imagine it'll take a while before it's all gone. I'm taking care of myself, though, don't you worry."

"All right, Dad." She swallowed. Obviously the situation had not been taken care of yet, but it had only been two days, and the police were probably still working on it. No doubt he wanted her to stay right where she was.

"Well, I'd better get back to the table."

They said goodbye and Nicky put the phone down. She would never make it as a spy or a secret agent. Never in a hundred years.

Dessert was being served as she came back to the table. Blake gave her a questioning look.

"I got hold of him, finally," she said, sitting down against next to him. "He said everything was under control."

Blake smiled. "Good. Feeling better?"

"A little. He didn't say much."

The conversation around the table continued and an hour later, dessert finished and coffee consumed, people said their goodbyes.

The road back to the house was pitch dark, but Blake was not fazed by the challenge of driving at night along the twisting road.

"When you spoke to your father, did he seem all right?" he asked.

"I think so. It's hard to tell. I felt like an idiot trying to talk in code, but he didn't say anything about my coming back to KL. I suppose the police are working on the case."

"It's only been two days."

"I know."

He gave her a quick sideways glance. "And to change the subject, what was it that you and Ghita were discussing? I take it you didn't tell her who you are."

Her pulse quickened. Alone in the car with him in the dark, she could not hide behind the presence of others. "No. As I'm sure you've noticed, she's quite enamored with you. As a matter of fact she was warning me off."

"I see." His voice was level, giving nothing away.

"This afternoon, at the pool, I overheard her and a friend discussing your many masculine charms."

"I'm flattered," he said dryly. "Did you go over and set them straight?"

"No, but I was tempted." He knew her so well. "Especially after they discussed how his wife must have been a moron." In the dark she sensed more than saw his smile.

"I can see it must have been a real challenge to keep your cool. How did you handle it?"

"I dove in the pool. The water was lovely."

"Very intelligent." He chuckled. "Then you found Ghita at the table with me on the veranda and when I left you couldn't resist getting back at her saying I invited you to stay with me at the house, suggesting, no doubt, long nights of romance and passion."

Her heart lurched at the image. "Well, yes," she said, trying to sound cool. "A bit adolescent, perhaps," she added with mature dignity. "If I caused you any problem, I'm sorry."

"You're not sorry, but never mind."

She grimaced in the dark. "Have you known her long?"

"Since she was a little kid. I knew her family when I was here as a Peace Corps volunteer, fifteen years ago, or whenever it was."

She felt an odd twisting of her stomach. That was longer than he had known her. Well, what did it matter? Nothing at all. She straightened in her seat.

"Why isn't she married yet? I thought in the Indian community parents arrange their children's marriages."

"Traditionally, yes, but not always anymore here in Malaysia. Her father tried, but has worn himself out arranging. Ghita refuses to cooperate. He told me he made the mistake of sending her to England for her education. It corrupted her beyond redemption, in his opinion."

"Meaning she wants to marry for love and pick out her own husband."

"Right. And we all know the success rate of those experiments." His voice was cool, yet she heard the faint note of bitterness hiding behind the businesslike tone.

Her stomach churned and the car was suddenly charged with painful emotion.

"I never thought of our marriage as an experiment," she said tightly, feeling defensive.

He shrugged. "You wrote me we didn't have a marriage at all."

Her nails were digging into her palms. She felt warm with nerves. "I suppose it was more like an... arrangement."

The silence was deafening. "I see," he said at last, his voice ominously low.

Her heart beat louder and louder. Something was happening to her, something frightening. "A convenient arrangement for you," she heard herself say. "You'd go on your trips and whenever you came home, I was conveniently there for you to cook your meals and be available in bed."

Again the silence, vibrating, pulsing.

He was staring straight ahead at the road. Anger radiated from him. She could feel it like a physical touch. She twisted her hands together in her lap, feeling as if there was no air to breathe, as if the dark forest outside the car was closing in on her. She stared blindly out the window, wishing she were a thousand miles away.

"I don't think," he said at last, "that this is a fruitful discussion." His voice was cold with barely restrained fury. "I have no desire to have an argument over something that's been dead and gone for over four years."

She had never heard him speak in that tone before and she felt a shiver go down her back. Her mouth was dry, her tongue paralyzed. It was just as well. Silence was the best answer, she was sure.

The rest of the way home neither one of them spoke another word. She felt overwhelmed by emotions—mixed up emotions sweeping through her like a wild, tempestuous storm, uprooting memories and images from the past.

Back in the house he poured himself a glass of whiskey.

"I think we need to clear up a few things here," he said. "You want a drink?" It was the first thing he had said to her.

She shook her head. All she wanted was to get away from him and the raw tension between them. "I just want to go to bed."

"In a little while. First, sit down."

"Don't order me around!"

He ignored her comment and took a drink from his whiskey. "All right. Let's take inventory of the situation. You and I are here together not by choice, but because of circumstances. I don't know how long you'll need to be here. A couple of days, a week, or—"

"A *week*?" It might as well be a year.

He shrugged. "Or maybe longer." He rubbed the back of his neck. "Considering our past relationship, this is certainly not an arrangement conducive to harmonious living. Don't think for a minute this is easy for me." He paused, hesitating, and a shadow passed across his face. "You were my wife," he said then, his voice ragged. "Now, every day, I look at you and am reminded of how it was between us, and how...wrong everything is now."

She tensed. She didn't want to feel, to be carried away by another maelstrom of emotions. "I'm sorry I'm causing you such hardship," she said tightly. "You just say the word, and I'll leave."

His jaw went rigid. "You're staying right here. What we need to figure out is how to act like two mature adults and make this situation bearable."

"What did you have in mind? We act like friendly neighbors? Brother and sister?"

"Whatever works to make it bearable."

She stared at him, her hands clenched by her side. "So what do you want me to do? Hide in my room, avoid being with you?"

He closed his eyes briefly and sighed. "No, of course not. Dammit, Nicky, I don't know."

"Well, how do you think *I* feel? I'm here against my will. For all practical purposes I am a prisoner in this house with no place to go, no clothes, no money, and I'm dependent on you for everything and you don't even want me here! You're just doing it for my father, and if he hadn't asked you, you could have just let me go after so bravely rescuing me and let me fend for myself!"

"And take the risk of something happening to you? For God's sake, Nicky, you were my *wife*. Do you think I don't care what happens to you?"

She swallowed. "I don't know. Why would you?"

He gave her a dark look, and she caught the glimpse of distress hiding in the shadows. Or was she just imagining it? "Never mind, Nicky," he said wearily. "Go to bed. It's late."

She lay in bed, wide-eyed, listening to the sounds coming from the forest. A cool breeze came in through the open windows and she pulled the thin blanket up to her chin.

Her body was restless, shivery, her nerves strung tight as if she'd overdosed on caffeine. It didn't make sense to feel so stressed out over something that had happened long ago, something that she had worked through and left behind.

Or had she?

I have no desire to have an argument over something that has been dead and gone for over four years. She heard again the cold fury in Blake's voice, saw his hands clenched hard around the steering wheel.

Dead and gone. Dead and gone. The words kept echoing in her mind. Her throat felt raw. She turned on her side, curled up in a ball and closed her eyes tightly. Blake's face swam before her mind's eye, a dark, intense look in his eyes. *You were my wife. Do you think I don't care what happens to you?*

She was aware of a terrifying need to hide, yet knowing she could not. The truth was clear and impossible to deny.

Anything that generated so much emotional energy wasn't dead and gone.

Something woke her in the middle of the night, but she wasn't sure what. Maybe a noise from some night creature, maybe a bad dream instantly repressed. It was a miracle she had slept at all—she hadn't expected it. She lay still, listening, but could not identify anything that might have awakened her. She sighed and changed her position, trying to keep her mind blank, trying to go back to the oblivion of sleep. Please, please, just let me sleep. No thoughts in my head, no words, no images... Count back from a hundred, slowly, see the numbers in your mind...

Her mind was not cooperating. It was going wild. It wanted to remember yesterday and last night, Ghita's face, the words she had said. The things Blake had said, the anger in his voice. It was hopeless. She tossed and turned, fighting the swirling kaleidoscope in her mind. *God knows what she must have done to him*.

What had she done to him? Nothing. She had loved him with all her heart. She had cooked wonderful meals. She had never complained about his work taking him overseas. She'd been an eager, happy lover.

She sat up straight in bed. She couldn't stand lying here in the dark any longer, fighting the demons. Maybe a cup of herbal tea would help; she'd seen various kinds in the kitchen. Maybe there was one good for chasing demons.

Tying a sarong around herself, she left the room and tiptoed down the corridor toward the kitchen. A strangled sound coming from Blake's room froze her in her tracks and her heart leapt in her throat. Had he called her name? Or was it just her imagination?

"Nicky..." Low, muffled, but unmistakable. The door was slightly ajar and she pushed it open quietly.

"Blake?" she whispered, apprehension clutching at her.

Silence. Then sounds of movement in the bed, a soft groan.

"Blake?" she repeated softly.

"What?" he muttered. A deep sigh. "Nicky, is that you?"

"Yes. You were calling me."

She heard him stirring in the bed, then a click, and the soft light of a small bedside lamp illuminated the room. He was semi-sitting up against the pillows, looking half-asleep and disoriented. His eyes were smoky gray, reaching for something unseen. He shook his head. His hair was disheveled.

"I was dreaming," he muttered, sounding confused.

"About what?" It was an automatic question.

He rubbed his face wearily. "About you."

CHAPTER SIX

HER breath caught in her throat as a tangle of emotions churned up inside her. Blake had been dreaming about her. She didn't know what to say, what to ask... afraid to ask. She stared at him in breathless silence.

"You were talking," he said, "but I couldn't understand anything you were saying. It was just... sounds, I don't know, like a foreign language, only it wasn't."

She was barely breathing. "What were we doing? Where were we?" she whispered.

"I'm not sure." He rubbed his forehead. "It's going. I can't really remember... just... it wasn't now. It was... we were still married." He closed his eyes tightly, as if trying to catch the dream inside, hold it in his consciousness. "You were wearing a red dress."

"A red dress? I never wear red." It clashed with the auburn of her hair.

He said nothing, his eyes still closed.

She found herself standing close to the bed; she must have moved further into the room without even knowing it.

"Where were we?" she asked softly. "At home?"

At home. How strange it sounded now.

He shook his head. "No—in a strange place. Dark, cold... I don't know." He shrugged, defeated. "It's gone." He straightened his back and raked both hands through his hair, frustrated.

She bit her lip, staring at his bare brown chest, feeling the silence pulsing around them. She hugged herself, feeling cold. "It was only a dream," she said, trying to dismiss it, knowing she could not.

He looked up, his gaze meeting hers for the first time since she'd entered the room. "You were very...distraught, angry." His mouth tilted in a faintly sardonic slant. "I wish I knew what heinous crime I had committed."

She swallowed. "It wasn't real."

He held her gaze, his eyes full of shadows. "You were so...distressed. It was...seemed very real to me."

She forced a smile. "Well, I'm not distressed now, so don't worry about it." She moved away from the bed, her legs unsteady. "I'm going to make myself some hot tea. Can I get you something?"

He shook his head. "No." Then he shrugged. "Oh, hell, I'm not going back to sleep now. I'll have some coffee."

"I'll get it." She left the room quickly, relieved to be away from the uneasy atmosphere between them.

Tea and coffee made, she put the cups on a tray and went into the living room. He was out on the veranda, leaning on the railing, staring off into the rain forest beyond the garden. She handed him his cup.

"Thanks." He gave her a rueful smile. "I'm sorry I woke you. I must have been talking in my sleep." He sounded calm, and quite awake.

"It's all right." She sipped the hot tea. "It's interesting out here in the night. It seems so mysterious."

"Yes." He took a drink of his coffee. "A universe onto its own. Millions of years old and it just keeps on going and growing."

The jungle throbbed and vibrated with sound. "It's so...alive," she said. "All these plants and animals and insects with their own role to play to keep the system going. It's all so...awesome, don't you think?"

"Yes."

She gave him a sideways glance. His face was amused, his mouth curved in a half smile. "What's so funny?" she asked.

"Oh, I was remembering you being awed by crocuses coming out of the ground."

"That's fascinating, too—the why and the how."

In the dark, his eyes met hers briefly, then he focused on the forest again. "It's what I always loved about you—your enthusiasm for the little stuff," he said quietly. "You made me notice things I'd never really paid attention to."

She remembered him laughing or smiling when she'd get excited about things. She remembered him teasing her.

"You used to tease me," she said softly, feeling a sudden painful sense of loss.

"You made me look at things differently," he went on. "You opened a whole new world for me."

His words made her feel light, almost dizzy. *You opened a whole new world for me.*

She closed her eyes and swallowed. "I didn't know you thought that." She heard the quivering of her own voice.

He was silent for a moment.

"I remember the first time I met you, at that party at your parents' house in Washington," he said then. "Here you were, looking elegant and beautiful in your long dress, telling me you loved to put on your hiking boots and go foraging for fiddleheads in the spring, and how delicious they were and how you had a special recipe." He gave a crooked grin. "And I had no idea what you were talking about."

"I remember." She smiled now, too. She'd explained to him that fiddleheads were the tender young shoots of certain wild ferns, still coiled and not yet spread out into their feathery, mature fronds.

"And I kept looking at you in your elegant dress sipping a glass of champagne and I couldn't for the world come up with an image of you in hiking boots and jeans prowling through the woods looking for fiddleheads."

It had taken him no time at all to come up with a solution to the problem. That very next day, a Sunday, they'd both been in the woods in search of fiddleheads.

She'd brought a picnic lunch in her backpack, and they'd been gone for hours. Magic hours. She'd been so exhilarated, so totally swept off her feet; it had all seemed so unreal, as if they'd been under a wonderful, magical spell, lost in a fairy-tale forest.

Sitting on a mossy log, he'd kissed her, as she'd known he would. All the hours and minutes that had led up to that kiss had been delirious anticipation. It had exploded in wild abandon and they'd both pulled back at the same time, as if by mutual agreement. As she'd gazed into his eyes, trembling with need, she'd known that something very special was happening, something more wonderful than anything she'd experienced before.

Memories. So many memories.

A soft cooing came from somewhere in the garden. A dove? She let out her breath slowly.

"Suppose there are fiddleheads in the woods here?" Blake asked, an odd note to his voice.

"I don't know...I suppose." Her heart was pounding. Her hand holding the teacup was trembling. She put it on a small table behind her, afraid she'd let it slip from her fingers.

Silence. He smiled at her, his face faintly illuminated by the moonlight and she saw the dark yearning in that smile and her heart lurched. He reached out and she felt his hands cupping her face and then he was kissing her, his mouth warm and urgent.

Her body flooded with warmth and all her senses sprang to life. His arms came around her holding her more closely, his kiss deepening, stealing her strength. Kissing him back, she soaked up all the familiar sensations, aching, wanting—feeling his body against her, wanting her. A soft groan came from his throat as he pulled away from her moments later.

"Come to bed with me," he said in her ear, his voice low and husky.

She was trembling in his embrace, aware that nothing more than two thin sarongs separated them. She couldn't make her voice work.

He trailed his fingers through her hair. "Nicky?" he urged.

She swallowed desperately, fighting the hunger. "I can't do this."

"Why not?"

"It's...it's not right." She sounded like a prudish virgin. She didn't know how else to say it, how to explain her fear. *I can't go back*, she thought, *I can't go back*.

He laughed softly. "We're both mature, unattached adults. We know each other well. We're alone and we need each other. Is that such a terrible thing, Nicky?"

She couldn't talk. She was groping for sanity, fighting the terrible yearning twisting inside her.

"Do you want me, Nicky?" he asked quietly.

"Yes," she whispered. It made no sense to lie. He knew her too well. The old magic was still there between them—the mutual enchantment of the senses, the sweet intoxication, the fires of passion. Her body still remembered, still reacted to him with familiar delight.

He knew how to touch her, how to make her body sing, how to make her feel alive and loved and special. He had always known that. The memories ached in her consciousness, suffusing her with naked need.

But lovemaking alone was not enough. It could not make up for other yearnings, other needs.

For tonight it will be enough, came a hungry little voice inside her. *Make love and forget the rest.*

Tears burned behind her eyes. "No," she said shakily. "It's not enough. I can't sleep with you just because... because it *feels* good. Because it would be so... so... *convenient*!"

She clenched her hands, feeling a swell of anger washing away desire, bringing back memories of the phone ringing in the empty bedroom. "Forget it! I'll be damned, if I'm going to be *convenient*!"

Her words throbbed in the silence, raw and anguished. He said nothing, a harshness edging his face as he looked at her with eyes suddenly filled with bitter anger. He took a step back, as if he could no longer tolerate her nearness.

"What the hell do you want, Nicky?" His voice was rough with emotion. "What the hell did you ever want? I gave you everything. Everything! And even that wasn't good enough!" He turned away abruptly and strode back inside.

She was shaking so hard, she was afraid to move. "Oh, no, Blake," she whispered into the throbbing darkness. "You didn't give me everything."

She had breakfast alone the next morning. Blake was in the office, writing. He came into the kitchen a while later as she was refilling her coffee cup and gave her a polite good morning, glancing at her for all of one second. He poured himself a cup of coffee, as well, and walked out without another word.

She wished she could just pick up her purse, get in a car and drive away. Only she had no papers, no car, no money and no place to go. She felt trapped and helpless, which made her furious. How could fate dare to do this to her, independent, self-reliant Nicky Arnell?

She left the kitchen, found paper, pen and research material in her room and went to the veranda to write.

Next time you find yourself kidnapped and held captive in the Malaysian jungle, try for a little culinary adventure to fill the long, empty hours. Go foraging for fungi. Jungle mushrooms come in a variety of shapes and colors, from skinny little white ones to large, fan-shaped orange ones. Unless all hope for eventual freedom has vanished, you want to select the nonpoisonous ones. Some varieties will make you feel sleepy and lazy, which may be desirable in your circumstances.

Marinate a pound or two of these sporophores in a liberal amount of lemon-flavored, extra-virgin olive oil to which has been added salt and pepper, three or four cloves of minced garlic and a handful of chopped fresh basil. Skewer them on thin, green bamboo sticks and roast gently over an open fire for about 10 minutes, or until tender, turning once.

If the Malaysian jungle is not available, you may substitute your local supermarket and purchase whatever type of fresh fungi is available within. You may use your backyard barbecue instead of an open fire.

There was no sign of Blake during lunch and she didn't see him again until dinner time. The tension during the meal was thick as smog. He hardly said a word and she made no effort at conversation. It was hard to swallow the food, but she made an effort so as not to worry or offend Ramyah.

Having served them coffee at the dinner table, Ramyah wished them good-night and left to go to her room.

"There's something I've wanted to ask you," Blake said, his voice low and contained.

"What?" Her throat felt dry as dust. She took a swallow of the hot coffee.

His eyes were smoky dark and unreadable. "What went wrong? I never understood what went wrong."

Her heart thundered in her chest. It was difficult to breathe. She knew what he was asking and anxiety rushed back with heightened intensity. "It...it just wasn't working anymore."

His right hand clenched around the coffee cup. "What kind of answer is that? *Why* wasn't it working?"

"We were never together anymore!" she blurted, her voice shaking. "You can't keep a marriage alive if you don't see each other!"

His jaw went rigid. "We had it worked out so we *would* see each other. It worked fine for the first year or so. Until *you* just weren't home anymore."

Under the table she felt her legs begin to tremble. She pressed her knees together. "I was there plenty of times! I was there *most* of the time!"

His jaw tensed. "But not when I was home." His voice was stone cold. "Not after the first year or so. Something happened, something changed."

Something had changed. In her mind, in her perceptions. What had seemed so good, had started to look different. She could feel again the old anguish, the old fear. And then suddenly anger overwhelmed her, and the need to lash out at him for all the pain he had caused her.

She faced him, clenching her hands in her lap. "It was all right for you to travel for weeks on end," she accused bitterly, "but *I* couldn't be gone? I was supposed to be home for you whenever you had time to grace the old homestead with your presence! And I did just that, the first year, didn't I? How convenient it all was for you!"

His jaw tensed into steel. His eyes were cold as ice. "It was not an arrangement *I* imposed on *you*," he countered, speaking the words in a slow, clipped manner. "It was a plan we made together for both of us!"

His anger and the wintry chill in his eyes almost frightened her. Warning bells clanged discordantly in her head but she was unable to stop herself. "But when the plan didn't work anymore," she went on, "when I wasn't home anymore to serve you hand and foot, you dropped me cold. You figured out something else. You didn't care if I came home or not! You could manage without me just fine!" Her voice shook. "You didn't need a wife!" She stopped talking, clenched her teeth together, feeling fragile, as if a mere breath of air would shatter her in a thousand pieces.

He scraped back his chair and swore viciously, his face a mask of anger as he looked down at her. "This is the craziest diatribe I have *ever* heard," he said with cold contempt. "Spare me!" He turned abruptly and strode out of the room as if he couldn't bear to be in her presence a moment longer.

She was left behind, sitting motionless in her chair as an aching emptiness took hold of her.

She had never thought of herself as a dutiful wife serving her husband, not until later, in retrospect, when fear and pain had created a new image to supplant the old happy one.

There hadn't been anything like old-fashioned duty in the way she had felt when he came home from his business trips. They were magic times, times she looked forward to for weeks while studying and writing and taking classes, trying hard to work ahead, to get done as much as possible so that when Blake came home she would have free time to spend with him.

She'd cook the most spectacular meals for the two of them, decorate the house with flowers and candles, burn incense, play romantic music, spray perfume on the bedroom lamp shades.

Many times they didn't even make it to the bedroom to make love...

She moaned, pressing the heels of her hands against her eyelids. It hurt so much to think about it, about those wonderful, wild, passionate nights when everything had been so right, so perfect between them.

It was all lost and gone, yet still it haunted her. She could not force away the images. She lowered her hands and sucked in a shuddering breath. Slowly she came to her feet and moved into the corridor to go to her room.

From the office came the steady clickety-clack of the computer keyboard. He was working again, writing his report, escaping from her. She dragged in an unsteady breath, her stomach twisting, thinking of the phone calls in the middle of the night, thinking of the phone ringing and ringing in their empty Washington town house.

At two in the morning she was still wide awake. She'd heard Blake go to his room an hour ago and the house was silent. She couldn't stand being in this house with him any longer.

She had to get away.

Now.

She was sitting up in bed, dressed in jeans and a T-shirt, as she had for several hours, and stared at the small bundle of her possessions she'd just stuffed in a plastic bag. It was pathetic; she felt like a refugee.

She tried to think clearly. Blake was asleep. He wouldn't hear her leave if she was quiet. The keys were in the Land Cruiser; she'd noticed him leaving them in the ignition. She still had his credit card. She'd drive back to KL, check into a hotel and call Nazirah. Nazirah could contact her father and get her passport and handbag and bring it to the hotel. It was all simple enough.

She slipped noiselessly out of the room, down the wooden stairs. She sat in the car, ready to turn the keys, feeling a moment of panic. It was pitch black all around. No traffic signs and no streetlights to help her out. Well, what could go wrong? All she had to do was follow the track for twenty minutes or so until she hit the village where the surfaced road would begin. This would lead to Paradise Mountain. From there it was a piece of cake to get back to the main road leading to Kuala Lumpur.

Holding her breath, she started the engine. It made a horrendous sound in the silence. What if Blake woke up?

Well, so what? He couldn't do a thing about her driving off, could he?

She drove away, seeing no lights come on in the house. She expelled a slow sigh of relief, yet not all tension was gone, she could tell. Her hands were clenched tight around the steering wheel as she maneuvered down the uneven track. She tried to relax. By the end of the day tomorrow she'd be on a plane out of the country. She should hold on to that vision.

Half an hour later she still had not reached the *kampung*.

Where was the village? Surely she should have reached it by now? Her eyes caught the fuel indicator and her heart made a sickening lurch. She was low on gas, but not out. Well, there was probably enough to reach Paradise Mountain and they had a pump there. Maybe there was even one before that. She still had a little cash left over from the money she had borrowed for her market expenses.

A while later she glanced at her watch again. Forty minutes had passed since she'd left the house. Her chest tightened with apprehension. She peered into the

darkness, hoping for a light somewhere to give an in-
dication of life. Nothing. The trail seemed even nar-
rower than she remembered. Maybe because it was night
and the forest seemed more oppressive.

Was she imagining it or were the headlights not as
bright as they had been? She moved on slowly down the
rutted track, soon realizing with a sense of horror that
the lights most certainly were getting dimmer and
dimmer. Realizing, too, that her foot on the accelerator
was hitting bottom while the Toyota was barely moving.
The fuel indicator was still telling her she was low, but
not out.

Something was wrong with the car.

She prayed she would see the village soon. She couldn't
possibly have missed it, could she?

The lights were very weak now and the surrounding
forest was getting darker and darker. The track was only
faintly visible in front of her and the car was hardly
moving at all.

In fact, it was dying.

CHAPTER SEVEN

MOMENTS later the Land Cruiser had died altogether. Nicky sucked in a deep breath and tried not to panic. In times of crisis you were supposed to keep a cool head and not panic. She knew that. She took in more air. Oxygen for the brain, that's what she needed.

Now, if only she knew something about cars... She could get out and have a look under the hood. No, she couldn't. It was pitch dark; she wouldn't see a thing. Anyway, she knew nothing about cars. The problem could be staring her in the face in broad daylight and she wouldn't know it.

She gave a tortured moan and dropped her head on the steering wheel. She had done it again. Her emotions had taken possession of her and here she was, stuck in the middle of nowhere in the middle of the night on a track in the Malaysian jungle. No lights anywhere, no houses, no paved road. What had happened to the *kampung*? She should have come right through the middle of it. It should be here somewhere! But there were no houses and not a sign of human life anywhere.

Maybe she had taken the wrong track. It would have been easy enough to do in the dark, only she hadn't seen another track before. All she'd been aware of was the one coming and going from the village to the house.

Tiny flashes of light flitted between the trees. Fireflies. Fireflies were comforting, but not the eerie shrieks and cries coming from the forest. She shivered. No way was she getting out of the car.

She was in trouble, deep, dark trouble.

Young American Tourist Perishes in Malaysian Jungle. She could see the newspaper headline clearly in her mind. If she had pencil and paper she could write the article herself and leave it for the reporters after they found her. She could give them all the juicy details on how she'd been kidnapped by her ex-husband, how torrid passion had flourished in the isolated mountain house, how she had tried to escape the terror of—

"Stop it!" she said out loud. "Stop it, you idiot. Do something constructive."

Like what?

Search the car for something useful. Whatever that might be. She groped for the glove compartment, opened it and fished around inside, finding, to her considerable delight, a flashlight. Not only just a flashlight, mind you, but one that actually had working batteries in it. Hope sprang up as she swept the light around the car's interior. Light! Never before had she been so happy to see light.

She searched through the vehicle, finding the car tool kit, but not anything for survival gear. Good Lord, it was irresponsible in an area like this not to— She stopped herself. She was hardly the one to talk about being responsible. Blaming others for their shortcomings was not going to help her now. Besides, everybody who normally used this vehicle wouldn't get lost. It was she herself who was to blame for doing something so brainless as to rush out in the middle of the night in a remote area like this.

It began to rain, a slow, steady downpour, splashing on the leafy greenery, drumming on the roof of the car. Well, she was dry. And cold. She hugged herself, shivering. How could it be so cold in the tropics?

She'd brought this upon herself. When her emotions got the best of her, she acted like an idiot. Oh, God, why couldn't she learn? Why couldn't she be more rational?

Once, years ago, she'd been an emotional wreck, too. She'd been alone, and it had been the middle of the night as well—a torpid summer night in Washington, D.C., when finally something inside of her had snapped. The fear and anxiety she had felt for months had changed into fury. She hadn't run away from Blake physically, then; he hadn't been home. She'd run away symbolically by writing a letter, a very short one.

The next morning, hyped up on coffee and rage, she had express-mailed it. For several days after that she had lived in a manic frenzy, her feelings yo-yoing between terror and hope, her thoughts filled with prayer and fear. At night she kept dreaming the dream, always the dream she didn't understand. Then Blake's answer had come by telegram: If That Is What You Want Do What You Need To Do Stop Blake.

She had stared at the words in shock, then slowly feeling had returned and the grief had been greater than she had been able to bear, too great even for tears. She'd pushed it back, fighting it, denying it until she'd learned not to feel. To be cold inside like an arctic lake.

And she had done what had to be done.

It had been easy. Forms were filled out, papers signed. All of it done without the two of them ever seeing or even talking to each other. Nothing to it. Easy as pie.

Except, when it was finally over, she'd been a divorced woman, and Blake was no longer her husband.

And she no longer dreamed the dream.

Nicky hugged herself and rubbed her arms. She wasn't very good at feeling helpless, but she couldn't think of anything useful to do except stay where she was and wait until morning. Maybe someone would come by. Maybe once it was light she should walk and follow the trail back to the house. She curled up in a ball and tried to sleep, but she was cold and uncomfortable and frightened and the spooky sounds coming from outside did not have a soporific effect.

The darkness stretched, time crawled. She was beginning to feel numb. In her mind, as a mental exercise, she wrote an article about her experience, trying valiantly for a touch of humor. Humor was not to be found. There was nothing remotely funny about sitting here in a primordial forest freezing and scared to death and wondering if you'd actually survive the ordeal.

The rain stopped, but the darkness was as impenetrable as ever. The air was damp and cold. She heard the hooting of an owl, or what sounded like an owl, a ghostly, lonely sound. She shivered. She longed for the dawn, for a human voice, for a cup of coffee. How long could one night last?

Then there was light flooding the car. And the sound of another vehicle, a sputtering engine laboring closer.

Moments later the door was wrenched open and the fierce beam of a flashlight shone on her face, blinding her. Instinctively she threw an arm across her eyes.

"What the hell are you doing here?" came Blake's voice, harsh and ragged—the most beautiful sound she had heard in all her life.

Relief flooded her, rushing warmth through her stiff body. "The car broke down," she managed to say, her voice sounding hoarse and shaky.

"How in God's name did you get it into your head to do a crazy thing like this?" His voice was rough with rage. "Driving away in the dead of night, driving away without putting gas in the car!"

"I'm not out of gas," she said hoarsely. "And don't you yell at me! Something is wrong with the car. It's dead. The lights went out and the engine quit."

"Where the hell did you think you were going?"

Her teeth were chattering. "To KL. To a hotel. I . . . I was going to ask a f . . . friend of mine to contact my father so we could figure something out."

Blake cursed under his breath. "Your father has enough to worry about right now!" He slammed the door and moved out of sight. A moment later he opened the other door and slid into the passenger seat. He handed her a thermos bottle. "Drink this," he ordered. There was no cup, so she drank it straight from the neck. It was coffee liberally laced with whiskey. Oh, God, and that on an empty stomach. It was not too hot and she gulped down a good quantity before handing it back. He took a few swallows himself and put it down.

She drew in a deep breath, clenched her hands in her lap and tried to look determined. "I'm not staying with you anymore!"

"You have no choice," he said harshly. "Don't act like a spoiled brat."

"I hate you," she said in a low, trembling voice, feeling close to tears, feeling helpless and unable to tolerate being at the mercy of this man. She wanted her money, her purse, her passport, her clothes. She wanted to get out—not only away from Blake, but out of the country, back to Washington, as far away as possible from him.

"I know," he said flatly. "God knows why. Here, have some more."

She drank more of the coffee, wincing as she slug-a-lugged it down. She couldn't stop shivering. She couldn't get warm.

"What the hell was I going to tell your father?" he demanded furiously. "That you found it necessary to escape in the middle of the night like some prison inmate? That you had perished in the damned jungle?"

She tightened her hands. "Don't exaggerate," she said, mimicking words he'd said to her a hundred times in the past. She was beginning to feel a little warmer, beginning to feel a little stronger. "I had no intention whatever to perish in the jungle." It sounded good. It sounded confident. As if she knew all the secrets of jungle survival. Which of course she didn't, but she was tired of his making her feel stupid. Not that she hadn't been stupid, but—

"Who do you think was going to find you here? And when?"

His autocratic behavior rallied all her defenses. She faced him, straightening her back and giving him a challenging look. "Maybe some *orang asli* hunters with blow pipes would have wandered by. They might have adopted me and I could have lived with them and learned their ways." Good Lord, where do I get this stuff from? she wondered, not able to stop herself. "Imagine the adventure!" she went on. "Then one day, some four or five years later, we would accidentally come across a Malay *kampung* and I would find my way back to modern civilization." She was warming to the subject, fueled by coffee and whiskey. "Just think about the book I could write then! I'd become famous! I'd go on talk shows and book tours. They'd make a movie out of the book and I'd become filthy rich! Just think about—"

He made a tortured sound—half groan, half laugh. "Oh, God, spare me your fantasies."

"It could happen! And now that you have found me, you're spoiling it all! Just go away and leave me alone!"

"Shut up," he ordered, pulling her roughly into his arms and kissing her fiercely.

She went limp in the warmth of his embrace. The comfort of his body so close, the strength of his arms supporting her disarmed the bravado that had fired her words. A sob broke loose, then another—big, heaving sobs she had no way to fight. He held her tightly, saying nothing, just holding her against him as if he were never going to let go of her again. She didn't know she had so many tears. They kept coming and coming from places she didn't even know existed. Tears of relief, tears of anger, tears of a bottomless grief.

"Oh, God, Nicky," he whispered in her ear when she'd finally stopped crying. "What am I going to do with you?"

He'd brought gas in a jerrican and poured it into the tank, but the car was unimpressed and refused to give any sign of life. They drove back to the house in the dilapidated pickup truck normally used for hauling tanks of cooking gas and other supplies.

"How did you know I was gone?" she asked, trying to see his expression in the dark.

He looked straight ahead, both hands on the steering wheel. "I woke up with a start. I had no idea why, except that I had this eerie premonition something was wrong. I couldn't figure out what. I tried to go back to sleep, but I couldn't. Finally, I got up and checked your bedroom and saw that you weren't there."

"And then you found the Land Cruiser missing," she guessed.

He nodded. "With very little gas left in it. I knew you hadn't filled it because there's a leak in the hose and there were no fresh spots. You wouldn't even have made it to Paradise Mountain, so I went tearing after you in this thing, but I didn't see you stranded anywhere. I knew the only thing that could have happened was that you'd got on the wrong trail before you even reached the village. And I was right."

She shivered and hugged herself. "I didn't know there was another trail. I hadn't seen it before, but I must have just taken it without even noticing."

"You'd only come that direction once and it's easy to miss the right track in the dark because of the angle it curves and the way the lights shine straight ahead onto this one."

"Where does it lead to?"

"Nowhere. It wanders around the mountain and turns back on itself. It's there for study and research."

He seemed his normal self again. He spoke calmly and without anger. Back at the house she had a warm shower and put on a terry bathrobe that belonged to Lisette.

Blake came into the corridor as she emerged from the bathroom. "I made you some mint tea," he told her. "Come along." He put his arm around her shoulders and propelled her into his bedroom right across from the bathroom. And she, like an obedient schoolgirl, allowed him to.

She glanced at the big rumpled bed, the air catching in her throat. A steaming cup of tea stood on the bedside table, the minty fragrance filling the room.

"Get under the covers," he instructed.

"This isn't my bed."

"No, it isn't." He pulled his T-shirt off over his head and tossed it on a chair. "Yours isn't big enough for both of us. I want you where I can keep an eye on you in case you decide to try and make another escape."

She stared at his bare chest. He couldn't possibly be serious. One bad mistake per night was about enough. She gave a short laugh. "You're just saying that."

"Yes, I am." He moved toward her and without ceremony unbelted her robe and pulled it off her shoulders. "Now get into bed and drink your tea." He held back the sheet and blanket and nudged her down matter-of-factly.

Her heart beating frantically, she sat up against the pillows and drew the covers up under her arms. He handed her the tea. She took it and sipped it, knowing this was crazy, knowing she should have just walked out and not allow him to take charge of her like this.

Knowing she was exactly where she wanted to be.

He stripped off the rest of his clothes without preamble. She looked at his naked body, that strong, familiar body—beautiful and aroused. Her heart lurched helplessly and it was suddenly hard to breathe. Her hands trembled as she lifted the cup to her mouth and sipped at the tea.

He got into bed next to her. He took the half-empty cup form her hands, put it down and switched off the light. Then he reached out and pulled her up against him as if it were the most ordinary thing to do.

Once, of course, it had been.

And even now, even with her mind going crazy and her thoughts in turmoil, even now it felt good and right. She fit against him as she had before: perfectly.

"When a woman is scared and cold," Blake murmured against her ear, "the best place for her to be is in the arms of a man."

The remark was totally uncharacteristic of him and she made a choking sound of surprise. "Mr. Chauvinist. And you're that man?"

"As far as I know, I'm the only one in the house."

"But I'm not scared and cold anymore."

"Then pretend you are."

"I don't want to make love to you," she muttered feebly. It was a lie, of course. Why else was she in his bed? Why else was she lying naked in his arms?

"Then don't. Just go to sleep." His arms tightened around her, pressing her closer yet against is warm, aroused body.

She gave a soft moan. "You're not serious."

"No, I'm not."

"You're trying to seduce me," she muttered, her lips brushing against the warm skin of his neck.

"I'm glad you're catching on." He eased his hold on her a little and lifted his head to look into her face. "And if you think this is convenient—if you think it's convenient for me to get shocked out of my skin to find you gone, to chase you in the dead of night in the middle of the damned jungle, not knowing where you are... if you think all that is a *convenient* way to get you in my bed, you'd better think twice."

Her lungs ached for air. She sucked in a shaky breath. "Then why bother?"

He groaned. "Because I want you. Because this situation is driving me crazy, and because I must have no pride at all."

Moonlight spilled through the open window, onto the bed, onto his face. She saw the faint grimace of self-derision.

"Pride? What does pride have to do with it?"

He gave a low, frustrated sound in his throat. "I don't want to discuss it. In fact, I don't want to talk at all. I don't even want to think." His mouth crushed down on hers, hot and urgent. There was a world of need and passion in that kiss—a need and passion reflecting her own. His body was tense and restless as it moved against her. He lifted his face away from hers. "All I want to do right now," he said huskily, "is kiss you all over and ravish you. But if you truly don't want to, Nicky, you'd better go now."

Her heart pounded wildly against her ribs. *Don't let him do this to you*, a little voice inside her warned. *Go! Now!*

She lay very still, gazing up at him, seeing the raw hunger in his eyes, a hunger contained by sheer force of will.

If she moved now, away from him, he would let her go. She was free to get up and leave the room. He didn't want her if she didn't want him. She realized she was barely breathing. Emotions clogged her throat. She wanted him more than she'd ever wanted him before—her body aching, yearning. She wanted his hands stroking and caressing her, his mouth kissing her all over. She wanted the fire only he had ever stirred up inside her. And she wanted to touch him and kiss him and feel his body tremble under her hands.

She wanted to feel that magical connection between them again, the wholeness of belonging.

"Nicky?" he said softly. "I know you well enough to know you want this, too. We both need this. We can't go on the way it's been these last few days. It's too damned . . . nerve-racking."

She nodded, pressing her face against his chest, feeling the hair tickling her mouth, her cheeks. That's why she had taken off in the middle of the night. Because she couldn't stand it anymore, because she was going crazy.

"And your running away from me is no solution," he added. "You know that."

"Yes," she whispered. "I—" Her voice faltered and tears filled her eyes.

"You scared the hell out of me, you know that?"

"I'm sorry," she said thickly. She fought against the emotion swelling inside. She felt his hand on her breast, a gentle touch that sent a fresh rush of tingling warmth through her.

"Nicky?" His voice sounded strangled. "Tell me what you want."

"I want us to make love," she said tremulously, pushing away everything in her mind—the memories of anguish and loneliness, the warning bells, the angry little voices.

Something broke loose in him—she felt the tremor pass through him, the easing of tension held in check with effort. No more restraint now as he kissed her mouth with reckless passion. No more restraint as he touched her breasts, kissing them one at a time, urgently, but never rough.

"I wished for this so much," he whispered. "So much."

"Yes." Her voice was barely a whisper. She ran her hands through his hair, feeling her breasts swell against his mouth. Her nerves tingled, her blood sang, her body danced.

She lost herself in the feelings, the freeing of inhibitions, touching and caressing his body all over, kissing him with an abandon fed by a fierce longing that no longer wanted to be repressed.

He whispered her name. "You feel so good, so good..."

She clung to him, drowning in a frenzy of need, letting herself go. Time and place receded, blurred, and she was aware of only him and the magic between them—the hunger that needed to be stilled, the wildfire that needed to be doused.

"Blake...oh, Blake..." a whisp of air, barely audible.

Hot skin against hot skin. Breath mingling with breath. Hearts throbbing. Tongues dancing. Hands searching, caressing. Again he moaned her name.

"I want you, I need you," he whispered. "I've missed you so."

"I missed you, too," she breathed, not thinking, only feeling. "So much, so much."

Their bodies locked together, they were swept high up into weightless rapture—a place where stars exploded and passion shattered until all that was left was a slow, languorous drifting and delicious contentment.

He kissed her cheeks, her eyes. "You're crying," he said huskily. "Oh, Nicky, please don't cry."

She smiled through her tears. "I'm just happy. It felt so right, so...so perfect."

"Yes." He hugged her convulsively. "Perfect."

*　*　*

She awoke in the morning sunlight, consciousness surfacing slowly. Cool air drifted in through the open window. Birds chirped. Gibbon monkeys whooped in the forest.

Drowsy with sleep, her body still heavy and sated, she sorted through wisps of thought and feeling. She felt so good, so good. Why was that? She remembered Blake's hands on her body. She remembered touching him. She turned and pushed her face into the pillow and smiled. Had it been a dream?

No dream.

She was in Blake's bed. A few hours earlier they'd made love. Wild, passionate love. He'd rescued her from the jungle, taken her home and into his bed.

She reached out her arm and hand and searched the bed. The sheets next to her were cool to the touch. She was alone. Where was Blake now?

Up already, working in the office, no doubt.

Slowly, the drowsiness faded. The room was bright with sunshine. It was time to get up; the night was over. So much light in this room. Nowhere to hide from reality. She closed her eyes against the light, but it did not bring back the happiness she had felt in the darkness of night as she lay wrapped in Blake's arms.

Well, he'd gotten what he wanted. A bitter thought, washing away sweetness and languor.

So have you, came a little voice.

Yes. And no.

She jerked herself upright in bed and rubbed her face. She'd wanted him, she wasn't going to deny it. He had given her a choice and she wasn't going to deny that, either. She'd wanted to be kissed again by him, feel his hands on her body, wanted his lovemaking and the way it always made her feel.

And like a miracle, it had happened just like that.

But you couldn't recapture the past. And sex was no answer to anything, no solution for real problems. She stared at the curtains fluttering in the breeze. She had wanted him so much, needed so much to feel loved and wanted, yet now in the new light of day, she wondered if love had had anything to do with what had happened between them.

"Oh, grow up," she muttered miserably. What had happened was not complicated at all. It was just like Blake had said: They had needed each other.

And in spite of the passion, they'd managed to be perfectly responsible about it. Or rather, Blake had been. Mature, responsible Blake, taking no risks.

Her chest ached. Part of her did not want to analyze what had happened in a dry, rational manner. A secret part of her wanted love and romance and the bonding of souls as well as bodies. It wanted desperately to find some meaning in the loving they had shared.

"Grow up," she said again, a little louder this time, trying to banish the longing from her heart. She swung her legs over the edge of the bed.

She found Blake working in the office and she stood in the door, feeling awkward.

She swallowed. "Good morning."

He glanced up at her. "Good morning," he returned.

He was waiting for a cue from her. She felt again the distance of time, the gaping void of four empty years between them, the old grief and anger—all of it still there in the brightness of daylight.

They looked at each other like strangers. She bit her lip, wishing she could think of something bright to say. She didn't know if she was angry or embarrassed or ashamed.

Ashamed. Why should she be ashamed? For expressing honest feelings and emotions? And what, exactly, was it that she had expressed last night?

Lust, pure and simple. It was her cool, analytical mind speaking, but it made her heart contract painfully. And what was so wrong with a little honest lust? It wasn't as if she'd picked the first man off the street and— No, she'd picked the first man she had ever truly loved. The man who'd been her husband. The man now sitting at the computer, observing her.

"Have you had breakfast yet?" she asked, for something to say. Her voice sounded shaky.

"Yes. I had something earlier." He pushed his chair back. "I need another cup of coffee, though."

"I'll get it for you," she offered. "I'll be right back."

He'd made a big pot and she poured a mugful and took it back to the office. She set it down on his desk and he lifted his head, searching her face.

"Are you all right?" he asked.

"I'm fine." She tried to sound businesslike. "Have you been up long?"

"About an hour."

As if by unspoken agreement, they made no further references to the night before, as if pretending it had never happened. Only it had, and the memory hung heavy in the air between them, full of unspoken emotions and unanswered questions.

"I apologize for taking the car last night," she said as they were eating the lunch Ramyah had prepared for them. "How are we going to get it back here?"

"I'll get Ali to go to Paradise Mountain and arrange for a tow truck to haul it to a garage."

"Do you know what's wrong with it?"

"From what you told me, it's probably the alternator and it'll need to be replaced."

"Is it something I did?"

"No. It would have happened anyway. You were just the unlucky victim."

Probably bad vibes. The car had not liked her. It had not wanted to be put to work in the dead of night. Who could blame it?

Apart from meals she saw little of Blake in the next few days. Whatever they'd thought to get out of their system, had only burrowed itself deeper. The thought of that passionate night haunted her, as if the very energy of it was still there. It was in her awareness every time she was near him. And she saw it reflected in his eyes, saw it still smolder there every time he looked at her. Even sharing their meals was a nerve-racking ordeal. Memories kept surfacing. A single word, a look, a sound, seemed to set them off. At night she stirred restlessly, her dreams confused and full of strange images she could not decipher.

It was a miserable situation. Three days later she was a worse wreck than before. She wrote, she read, she prowled through the house. Blake kept himself hidden in the office.

The Land Cruiser had been hauled away and was returned to the house a few days later in fine working order.

"Tomorrow I'm going to KL for the day," Blake announced at dinner that night. "I have a meeting about the project, and I'll go see your father and figure out what's going on."

Hope leapt joyfully. "I'll come with you!"

"No, you are not," he said flatly. "It's too risky, Nicky. We don't know what's going on and it makes no sense to put you in danger. We don't know if the police caught those gangsters or if they're still hoping for a chance to grab you. You're staying right here."

"Don't tell me what to do!" She sounded like a child, but it seemed it was the only defense she had. Blake was right, of course. They had no idea what problems her father was having with those Hong Kong criminals. Attempted kidnapping was no minor offense. Her own discomfort should not be a major consideration, even if she was going demented in the process. If she used her brain, she knew that staying right here was the best course of action.

She just didn't like it. She hated it.

"I'm sorry, Nicky," he said, "but there's no choice. If your father says you can come back, I'll drive you back to KL the next day. In the meantime, I'll give him a message, if you like."

She tensed. "Tell him I'm on the verge of losing my mind and I want to get out of here. Tell him I want my purse and my passport!"

"Anything else?" he asked calmly.

A dose of rat poison, she almost blurted. "My notebook and computer disks," she told him instead. "My father knows where they are. And I want some clothes."

He nodded. "Now, one more thing." He pushed his empty plate aside, leaned his arms on the table and looked straight into her eyes. "I've rescued you from an uncertain fate twice in the last few days," he stated. "Twice is my limit. So do me a favor and don't do anything stupid while I'm gone."

She gritted her teeth. "You sure know how to give orders, don't you?"

He gave a long-suffering sigh. "Please promise me you'll be careful. Don't go wandering off into the forest. Don't come up with some other compulsive scheme to—"

"I get the picture," she snapped. "I'll wait for you to talk to my father and get my money and my passport. Then I'll get out of here."

He flashed her a dark, unreadable look, but made no comment.

He'd already left when she awoke the next morning. He'd started early since it was a long drive and he intended to come back the same day. It was a relief to have the house to herself. She felt as if she could breathe again.

Oddly, the day seemed to stretch forever, in spite of her having plenty to do. There was reading, researching, writing. Blake had given her his laptop computer to use, saying he could use the O'Connors' PC in the office.

He told her he'd be home by eight, but by nine he still wasn't back. Well, he was probably delayed for some reason or other, and there was no phone to let her know.

By the time it was ten she was beginning to worry. What if something had happened? What if he'd been in an accident? Her mind created images and scenarios, all involving blood, broken bones, and worse, which did nothing at all to calm her nerves. She brewed a second pot of tea and tried to read, doing research for an article about love potions and aphrodisiacs, but no matter how absorbing she'd find this under normal circumstances, it could not compete with the frightening images rampaging through her mind.

She stared out into the throbbing darkness. She was sitting on the veranda amid the smoldering mosquito coils, awash in tea and terror, waiting. Oh, God, she couldn't stand waiting.

It was close to eleven when the headlights finally swung through the yard and across the verandah. Fear ebbed out of her chest, and with it came again the old sense of déjà vu—a wisp of awareness fluttering out of her subconscious. And then she knew, suddenly, as if a light had been turned on in her memory.

The dream. It brought back the feelings in the dream.

Blake came bounding up the stairs with amazing energy. He looked wonderful—strong, vibrant, and very much alive. His brows arched in surprise as he noticed her. "Hi," he said. "Thought you'd be in bed by now."

"Where were you? What took you so long?" She sounded like a worried wife, and it didn't escape him.

He gave her a crooked smile as he dumped a box and his briefcase on the veranda floor.

"Missed me?"

Annoyance replaced her worry. "Heck no, I had a wonderfully peaceful day."

"I thought you might." He made a move toward the living room. "I'm having a drink. Can I pour you one?"

"No, thanks. I'm swimming in tea."

He was back a moment later and leaned back against the railing, apparently not ready to sit down again after his long drive. "I'm sorry I couldn't call you and let you know I was going to be late. The man I had to see had some sort of a crisis and I couldn't meet with him until late this afternoon, so I couldn't get out of town until almost seven." He took a long drink from his whiskey. "Your father is all right. The contract has been canceled and he's managed to get the attention of some high-powered Hong Kong officials, who are taking a close look at that fraudulent company."

She let out a sigh. "Good. Did the police figure out who came into the house and destroyed my room?"

"They know the people who were behind it, but they haven't been able to find them, which is cause for concern." He frowned. "Your father is concerned they may be out for revenge now, which would be rather stupid on their part, but they haven't shown great brain power to start with, so it's something that needs to be considered."

Her heart sank. "And what does that mean? That I can't go back to KL?"

"Right."

"This is crazy! How long is this going to take?"

"I have no idea. Your father will let us know."

"And I'm just supposed to accept this? I'm supposed to just hang out here in the middle of nowhere for God knows how long? Couldn't he have figured out something else?''

Blake shrugged. "He feels you're safe here."

She gave a frustrated groan and dropped her face in her hands. "Oh, God, I'm going crazy."

"No, you're not," he said calmly. "You're tough."

But not tough enough. She was going to get out of here one way or another. She lifted her face. "Did you bring my stuff?"

He gestured toward the box. "Your clothes and handbag are in there." He put down the glass, reached for his briefcase and opened it up. "Here you go," he said, reaching in. "Notebook, computer disks, and traveler's checks." He put them on the table as he called them off. "No passport."

Her heart lurched. "No passport? It was right there in the desk drawer with the traveler's checks and the disks!''

"Obviously, somebody took it."

"This is crazy! You mean to say those mafioso actually went into my father's office and stole it out of the desk drawer?''

He snapped the briefcase shut. "You can apply for a new one, but it will have to wait till it's safe to go back to KL.''

Anger rushed to her head. "I don't want to wait! I want to leave! I want to get out of here!''

He took a leisurely drink from his glass. "Sometimes, we can't have what we want," he said levelly. "I realize it's not always easy to accept, especially not for someone spoiled and indulged like you.''

She gasped. "What? You call me spoiled and indulged?''

He raised a quizzical brow. "Surely that's not a new revelation to you?''

She was beyond words.

He took another swallow of his whiskey. "Has there ever been anything you wanted and didn't get?" he asked conversationally.

Heat rushed through her body, rose to her head. "Oh, yes, there has been," she snapped, the words spilling out like hot coals. "A happy marriage, to mention one!"

CHAPTER EIGHT

THE atmosphere turned instantly electric. Her words hung in the air, throbbing, threatening. Blake's face had turned to stone and his eyes did not leave her face.

"As far as I know," he said with slow emphasis, "we had a happy marriage up until you decided not to be home with me anymore. And may I remind you that you are the one who left me, that you were the one who wanted the divorce?"

No! she almost shouted. *You're all wrong! I didn't want it at all! All I wanted was for you to wake up!*

She'd asked for the divorce, but she hadn't wanted it.

"And you did *not* want it?" she asked with bitter mockery. "Remember how long it took you to sign the damned papers? The lawyers had them back by return of mail! I imagine it took you all of one lousy minute to sign them!"

His eyes narrowed. "What had you expected? That I would force you to stay with me against your will?"

It wouldn't have been against my will! All I wanted was for you to tell me you loved me and needed me and didn't want to lose me!

He shook his head slowly. "I didn't want a woman who didn't want me. If I remember correctly, we hadn't seen each other for four or five months when you wrote me that lovely little note."

"You were out of the country!" she said wildly. "You were always out of the damned country!"

"My work takes me overseas, you knew that, and I was home between assignments for weeks on end, exactly when I said I would be, give or take a day or two." His jaw was hard as steel. "Every time I came home, you were not. You had one excuse after another."

Excuse. Anger burned inside her. It had never seemed to her that he cared one hoot that she wasn't there. He'd never told her he wanted her home, never told her he missed her. "You sure didn't seem to care!"

A silent moment. "Oh, no," he said slowly, "you, my devoted ex-wife, were the one who didn't care enough to be home when I was, the way we'd planned it from the beginning. What sticks in my mind specifically is your New York jaunt." His eyes bored into hers. "Remember that one?"

It had been one of the most miserable times of her life, vivid still in her mind. "Yes, I do," she said between clenched teeth.

"You came back from Sophie's in Rome while I was in Guatemala and the day before I came home you took off to New York for a *cooking course*. We hadn't seen each other for four months by then. *Four months*," he repeated harshly, "and you had to take a *cooking course!*"

"You could have come to New York for the weekend."

He gave a bitter, mocking laugh. "Oh, thank you for your generosity!"

"If you cared so much, then why didn't you?"

Clenching his hands, he shoved them into his pockets. "You didn't ask me! I assumed you had other plans. If you cared so much, why did you go in the first place? No, darling, don't you dare talk to me about caring! You made it abundantly clear you didn't care to be married anymore. You were the one who wrote that lovely little note to me about how our marriage wasn't working and you wanted out."

"And it bothered you so little, you didn't even pick up the phone to talk about it with me!"

One dark brow rose in a mocking arch. "All you thought it was worth was a *letter*. You didn't even bother to wait for me to come back home so we could talk about it in person. You wrote me a lousy little *note*! And going by those few concise lines, I gathered there was no point discussing it. You were very clear." He gave her a stony look. "And I see no point discussing it now, after all these years." He glanced at his watch. "It's been a long day and I'm tired. Good night."

You were the one who didn't care to be married anymore. His words floated through her mind all through the night as she stirred restlessly in semi-sleep.

She didn't see him again until lunchtime. She'd have preferred to eat alone, but didn't want to cause Ramyah any extra work. Blake was aloof, but polite. The air was charged with emotion, the tension between them like a living presence at the table with them.

"I stopped by the Patels' on my way out yesterday," he commented, breaking the silence. He spooned dressing over his salad. "We've been invited to dinner on Saturday night."

The Patels. Ghita's family. And he apparently expected her to go with him. She concentrated on a piece of lettuce on her plate. "You should probably go alone," she suggested. "I have no business being there."

"You were invited," he stated flatly. "Don't offend them by not showing up."

If she didn't want to go, she didn't have to go, but she recoiled from being childish about it and coming up with headache excuses. A dinner party might be fun. It would do her good to be around other people, and the food, spicy, Indian food, would be wonderful, no doubt.

She went back to her own writing after lunch. She stared at the books of love potions and aphrodisiacs.

She'd spent all morning reading and taking notes. It was time to do some writing.

> *If ever you find yourself in the unfortunate situation of being all alone in an isolated house with your ex-husband, you may want to reconsider food as something you merely eat to sustain life or consume for the sheer epicurean pleasure of it.*
>
> *Food may serve other purposes.*
>
> *In a recent article I suggested using food as a means to character analysis. Today I want to highlight other purposes. Obviously, in the stressful situation mentioned above, it will soon occur to you that food may be used as a weapon: You can poison your ex and be rid of him forever. This is, shall we say, distasteful, not to speak of illegal, and I will therefore not linger on it, or give recipes—although I do have a few.*

Nicky closed her eyes and stopped typing. Good Lord, where was this stuff coming from? Don't think, just type, she told herself and, taking a deep breath, she returned her attention to the keyboard.

> *Let us consider a more positive, if fanciful, possibility. Imagine, just for the sake of it, that by some inexplicable cosmic magic, your ex-husband has become a changed man—a dream man in fact. And now you want to win him back. Remember, this is a fairy tale, and what's wrong with fairy tales once in a while?*

Nicky's fingers stopped moving and she took in a shaky little breath. What was she doing here? How did she make up this stuff?

No time to think. Later. Finish this first. Pushing out rational contemplation, her hands went flying again.

This dream man is not interested in you at this point, so your goal is to make him notice you and fall passionately in love with you all over again. Food can be your ally. I'm sure you see where I'm going with this: straight to the magic of love potions and aphrodisiacs.

She stopped to consult her notes, leafing through the notebook, then checking a recipe in one of Lisette's books.

To start with, in the afternoon, make him a nourishing shake of camel's milk, dates and honey. If you've read your Arabian literature, you will know this works.

She was going strong. It was a wonderful feeling to be absorbed, for the words to just come out. She kept referring to her notes and the books, recording strange recipes from exotic corners of the world. For all the bizarre concoctions she described, she supplied alternative recipes more agreeable to the modern American tastebuds: Shrimp in Ginger-Ginseng sauce, Spiced Apricots with Toasted Almonds. In fact, they were so agreeable that her tastebuds began to beg for something rich and flavorful.

She found it in the kitchen: a perfectly ripe mango. She peeled it over the sink and put her teeth into it, juice dripping down her hands and chin. It was delicious—a veritable orgy of tastebud-titillating flavor.

At this exact moment, Blake sauntered into the kitchen and witnessed the spectacle.

"I hope you are enjoying that," he said dryly.

With her mouth full of the fruit, she was incapable of offering more than a grunt in answer. By now the juice had reached her elbows and she was only half finished. She put the mango on a plate, turned on the water, and washed off.

"My I suggest an alternative method of eating the rest?" he asked, humor coloring his voice.

It was a relief to hear the humor; his anger must have dissipated. She took a towel and gave him a breezy smile. "No, you may not." She found a fork and knife, and took care of the remaining mango in a more decorous manner while he watched her with annoying interest.

"It tastes better the other way," she announced, sounding faintly like a rebellious child.

"It had more entertainment value, too," he commented. "You and your passion for food have always been amusing."

"My passion for food is serious business," she stated haughtily. "I make my living with it. Also, I'm learning new things all the time. Do you want to hear what I know about mangoes?" Good heavens, why was she doing this?

She was doing this because having a lighthearted conversation was much easier on the nerves than anger and bitterness. And her nerves needed soothing.

He sat down at the kitchen table and stretched out his legs. "By all means, tell me what you know about mangoes."

Apparently he was in need of some nerve-soothing conversation, as well.

She rinsed the plate and put it in the sink. "Well, to start with... Do you know that Buddha had a whole grove of mango trees? He would sit in the shade to meditate. Now, if that is not serious, I don't know."

He nodded solemnly.

She sat down across from him. "Then, there was a Hindu god, Subramanya, who got so upset when he couldn't get a mango that he wanted, that he renounced the world."

"That's taking your mango seriously. What else?"

She waved her hand. "I'll leave it at that." It didn't seem appropriate to discuss the aphrodisiac qualities the mango was believed to have by men in the East. "The rest is probably not too interesting for you," she said casually and examined her nails.

"How's your writing going?" he asked.

"I'm doing well," she stated, not sure that this was true. On rereading, she might want to toss it all in the wastebasket. "I got so hungry, I had to take a break."

He nodded. "I can see that. Considering your profession, I can't imagine why you're as slim as you are."

"I only eat good stuff."

His mouth quirked. "Right. Mocha mousse with whipped cream, and the like."

"That's for special occasions only." She felt a hard knot of pain in the pit of her stomach. Special occasions like homecomings and wedding anniversaries.

He gave a half smile. "Don't feel you have to wait for a special occasion—if the spirit moves you, make us some mocha mousse one night."

"Without a special occasion, the spirit won't move," she said curtly and came to her feet. "I'm going back to work."

He stood up, as well, and as she moved past him he reached out and pulled her into his arms. It all happened so fast, it stunned her for a moment. Then her body registered what was happening and was instantly aflame.

He kissed her with a crushing heat—as if he wanted to impress himself on her, brand her with his need. There was a desperation in that kiss, drawing from her an instinctive response. She leaned into him, yielding to him.

A timeless moment later he released her abruptly, and she grabbed dizzily for the counter to support her.

"Go back to work," he said gruffly. "Snack time's over."

* * *

She stared at the computer screen, suppressing a hysterical little laugh. Here she was, writing an article about a love feast, about aphrodisiacs and love potions.

She had to be out of her mind. The last thing she should be concentrating on was the stirring up of sexual desires.

All she had to do was look at Blake and her pulse would speed up. All Blake had to do was kiss her or touch her and her body reacted automatically, instinctively, as it always had, from the very moment she had met him. Even now, in spite of all the unhappiness that separated them, the electric pull, that magical magnetism drawing them together was still there.

No aphrodisiacs necessary. No love potions required.

She gathered the papers and books and dumped them on a shelf to make room on the desk. What she needed to do was write her article on street food, work out her notes about the day she had spent in the markets and streets of Kuala Lumpur with Nazirah. No love involved—no writing about surging passions, sensual desires and erotic pleasures.

She worked all afternoon, not emerging from her room until dinner was served.

"Ramyah is off on Friday." Blake told her as they sat down at the table. "It's the Muslim holy day. She wants to know if there's anything in particular you'd like to eat so she can fix it tomorrow and leave it in the fridge for us."

Nicky spread the napkin on her lap. "She doesn't need to do that. I'll be happy to cook," she said without thinking. "I need something to do besides reading and writing." And getting into emotional arguments with you, she added silently.

He nodded. "Fine."

To her considerable relief they managed to eat dinner without tense conversation and toxic accusations.

After Ramyah had finished in the kitchen, Nicky went exploring in the freezer, fridge and pantry to contemplate the possibilities for Friday dinner. There were frozen salmon steaks, which were tempting, and a frozen duck. Ah, she could do wonders with a duck! So could the Chinese, she remembered. Endless love recipes, as a matter of fact. Well, she wasn't concocting any love food—just a nice dinner. She put the duck in the refrigerator so it would thaw slowly over the next thirty-six hours or so.

They avoided each other on Thursday. Blake stayed in the office working most of the day, and she was in her room writing most of the day. He seemed to have as little appetite for further emotional skirmishes as she did, which was no surprise. Blake was a calm, rational person who solved problems in a calm rational manner. The anger she had witnessed this past week had surprised her.

And his passion.

It was in his eyes, in his face—a deep, smoldering struggle.

She took a deep breath and focused on the empty computer screen in front of her. Her problem was that she was thinking about love too much. She should be working. She called up the street food article and reread what she had produced earlier that day.

Snakes. That's what she should be thinking about—a bin full of snakes.

All day Friday she had the kitchen to herself. It was a joy to do some cooking again and she found herself humming a cheerful tune as she was chopping lemon zest, stopping in the middle when she found Blake standing in the door, watching her, his eyes full of dark shadows.

Her heart made an odd little leap. "Can I get you something?" she asked, for something to say.

"No, nothing. I just need a drink. He moved towards the fridge, took out a bottle of white wine and poured himself a glass without asking if she wanted any. He then proceeded to knock the glass over, spilling the wine all over the countertop. Muttering something unintelligible, he took the dish sponge and mopped up the spill.

"What's wrong?" she asked.

"Nothing," he said tersely. Tossing the sponge in the sink, he turned away abruptly and marched out of the kitchen without a drink.

She went on mincing the lemon zest, trying not to let the incident spoil her good mood. She was enjoying herself. She inhaled the fresh fragrance of lemon. Ah, it was going to be good.

And it was.

Everything was perfect. She'd found candles and flowers and a pretty tablecloth. Lisette had not disappointed her. For all her common sense cotton clothes, she was a sensualist, too—the food in the pantry, the poetry books on her shelves, and the wonderful collection of music all attested to that.

Nicky glanced at the beautifully set table, the flowers, the candles, feeling a sudden trepidation. What was she doing here?

She'd gone all out, like she always had.

She closed her eyes. Why? Why had she done that?

She stood very still, knowing the answer, admitting the truth to herself, finally.

She loved Blake, still. She had always loved him, and there was nothing she could do about it. A painful sense of inevitability took hold of her.

Opening her eyes, she surveyed the table once more. She could take the candles away, move the flowers to the coffee table. She struggled with herself, then slowly turned away, leaving the table as it was.

Blake was on the veranda, reading. A novel, she noticed. "Dinner is ready," she announced.

"I'm coming."

She went back to the kitchen, took the duck from the oven, sprinkled chopped cilantro over it and brought it to the table.

"Ah, a royal repast," Blake said as he sat down. He smiled. "Not that I expected anything else, of course."

"I had all the time in the world," she said lightly, "being kidnapped and held captive in the deep dark forest."

"I did not kidnap you. I rescued you."

"Right." A strange feeling gripped her. She remembered his carrying her in his arms, recalling the odd sense of dèjá vu. "I had a recurring dream about you rescuing me," she said on impulse, "a long time ago."

He poured the wine. "Rescuing you from what?"

"I have no idea." She served herself some herbal rice and handed him the bowl.

"When did you have that dream?"

"When we were still married." She glanced away. "It was a strange dream."

"And you still remember it?" He picked up the platter with the pieces of duck resting in lemon-papaw sauce and held it so she could serve herself.

She nodded, biting her lip, regretting having mentioned the dream. She didn't want to talk about it. He must have sensed her reticence because he dropped the subject, asking if she'd read the book he'd just started this afternoon.

They talked about books, about music, about the work he had done two months ago in Mozambique. He was talking, keeping up his end of the conversation, and she

wondered if he was conscious of it, doing it to be cour-
teous, because, after all, she had spent much effort preparing the food, or if it was just happening naturally.

The meal was delicious and he ate with appetite, taking
a second serving of the duck. "You haven't lost your
touch," he commented, smiling at her. "This is
wonderful."

Her heart gave a little leap of pleasure. "Thank you."

He was still looking at her, and she felt a slow heat
begin to rise inside her, a quivering awareness of something more behind his words. She dropped her gaze to
her glass, picked it up and took a drink of the wine.

The tape she'd put on the stereo clicked off, filling
the room with silence. Blake pushed his chair back. "I'll
get it."

He put on another tape, sat down again and turned
his attention back to his food. Melodious strains of
Spanish guitar music drifted through the air. She glanced
at his hands cutting the duck. Such nice hands. She took
in a slow breath and searched for something to say.

"Why were you angry earlier, when I was cooking in
the kitchen?" she asked.

He looked up. "I wasn't...angry," he said quietly.
"Seeing you there in the kitchen, enjoying yourself
cooking...it brought back memories."

Her heart contracted. Memories, always memories.
Everything they said or did brought back memories.

"I remember coming home after a trip," he said then.
"I remember looking forward to coming home and
finding you in the kitchen, cooking, a lacy apron on,
your face flushed. You so enjoyed doing it, and I so
enjoyed seeing you this way—not because I'm an old-
fashioned male wanting his woman in the kitchen in a
subservient way, but because you made an art out of it."

"Yes." She tried to give him an easy smile, but her
mouth felt stiff.

"You did it to please me," he went on. "To make me a home-cooked meal after all the restaurant fare I'd had for weeks on end." He paused. "I loved seeing you cooking because you did it because you loved me." Painful, aching longing in his voice, his face.

She felt a tightness in her chest. It hurt to hear him say those words, to see the pain of memory in his face. Or was she just imagining it? Was it only her own emotions she was transposing?

The music throbbed softly, sensuously. She put her napkin next to her plate. "I'll get dessert." Her voice sounded unsteady and she went into the kitchen, taking in a shuddering breath as she leaned her forehead against the coolness of the refrigerator. It had been a mistake to cook this meal, to call up the memories.

I loved seeing you cooking because you did it because you loved me.

She took in a steadying breath and straightened away from the refrigerator. She was not going to go to pieces. She was going to get the dessert, go back to the table and change the subject. Say something funny and frivolous.

She moaned. How was she going to do that? Well, she'd think of something. Opening the refrigerator door, she took the two dishes of ginger *bavarois* off the shelf and nudged the door closed with her elbow. Turning around, she saw Blake coming into the kitchen.

He took the dishes from her, looking into her eyes. "Let's have this later," he said softly.

Her heart lurched. Another home-coming ritual: dessert in bed, after they'd made love.

Her throat went dry. Even here she could hear the hypnotizing music floating in the air and she felt herself begin to tremble. He put the dessert back in the refrigerator, his eyes not leaving her face. He closed the door and put his arms around her.

"I want you," he said huskily. "I keep on wanting you all the time. Please tell me you want me, too."

Soft words, stirring her blood, quickening her pulse. No air to breathe. Her head felt light and her knees trembled. Too much wine with dinner. No resistance. Too many memories of love and passion. So much longing and yearning inside her. Her body aching, wanting.

It wasn't the wine. It was a different enchantment, a spell that could never be broken. She closed her eyes and sighed, sliding her arms around him.

"I want you, too," she whispered.

She loved him. She loved him so.

CHAPTER NINE

THEY were in his bedroom, she realized moments later, not knowing how they'd made it there—floating on air, maybe. He began to take off her clothes, slowly, kissing her skin as he exposed it little by little—her breasts, her stomach, her thighs, stirring up inside her a feverish warmth—delicious, agonizing. Her hands shook as she helped him with his clothes, sliding her hands across his bare skin, touching soft hair and hard muscles. With a low groan he picked her up and gently lowered her onto the bed, as if she were fragile and precious, and she felt a sweetness flow through her like warm honey.

He leaned over her and looked at her for an endless moment, silent, just looking. There was a tenderness in his eyes that made her body tremble. Something soft and fragile began to glow inside her—something beyond the need of her body.

He lowered his mouth to hers, kissing her slowly, sensuously, as if he had all the time in the world, as if he wanted it to last forever. His tongue danced a slow waltz with hers, retreated, stroking her lips, teasing. He moved lower, trailing kisses, while his hands feathered along her skin, making her body sing, filling her head with starlight. She made a small sound in her throat, reaching out to touch him, too, moving a little to gain better access.

She reveled in the feel and taste of his body, that wonderful body that was all hers now, and he took her hands and gently put them away from him. "Just be," he whispered. "Just let me touch you for now."

It was like floating in music, tasting color and touching waves of golden light. It was like not feeling her body, feeling only sensations, wondrous sensations.

"This feels so good," she murmured, "so good."

She felt his smile against her breast. "And it's going to feel better yet," he promised.

She wriggled beneath him, skin sliding across skin. "Are you sure?"

He laughed softly. "Oh, yes I'm sure."

And he went on to create his magic, and she went on drifting in sensual sensations that knew no time and place, that filled her every cell until she was so full, so full of exquisite pleasure she could no longer keep it for herself.

She lifted her arms and pulled his face to hers, sliding her lips against his. "I want...I need to touch you," she whispered breathlessly.

And she touched him, creating new pleasures for herself as well as for him, and they clung together in breathless need, melding together in a dance of rapture, faster and faster, up to the edge of passion where they trembled, lost the rhythm, and tumbled together through a heaven of bliss.

She drifted into consciousness slowly, lazily, aware of a wonderful sense of well-being. The bed was comfortable, the morning air wafting through the windows clean and fresh.

An arm touching her.

Stop the floating upward. There was danger waiting on the surface. She wanted to stay down, to feel the warmth and dreamlike trance—a space in her mind where there was no time and place, only sunshine and the joyous sense that all was right and euphoric.

She snuggled against the warmth, feeling him stir against her, reaching for her. His hand on her breasts, his mouth kissing her.

Drifting. Floating slowly back into paradise.

Afterward she thought it must all have been a dream and she didn't want to wake up.

"Don't get up," Blake whispered, kissing her softly. "I'll bring you coffee."

The words touched the fringes of her consciousness, lingering. Familiar words. Familiar voice. She smiled into the pillow, delicious languor pervading her body. She didn't want to open her eyes.

Later there was bright sunshine and the sounds of birds singing. The smell of freshly brewed coffee. She kept her eyes closed and sighed. It was good here in the big bed. She savored the feeling of drowsy contentment—her body felt so whole, so...sated. She stretched a little and sighed again lazily.

Laughter, low and amused. "Wake up, you slothful woman. Here's your breakfast."

She gave a low moan of protest and opened her eyes. Blake stood by the bed, a *kain* wrapped around his hips, a tray in his hands. It took an effort to move into a sitting position. She covered her mouth and yawned.

His eyes held amusement as he deposited the tray on her lap, and leaned forward to kiss her. His mouth was warm and firm, his tongue teasing her lips. "Are you awake?"

"Mmm...I think so. I smell coffee."

He chuckled and straightened away from her. She glanced down, taking in the cup of strong, milky coffee, the golden French toast swimming in honey, the sliced papaya. "Oh, wow," she said. "Nobody has fixed me breakfast in bed in years and years." Only Blake had ever done that.

Only Blake.

She glazed at the tray on her lap, remembering again the mornings he'd brought her breakfast, remembering all the nights of their married life when everything between them had still been good, when she had felt loved and whole.

Remembering last night.

Shades of yesteryear, when love had been real.

She was sitting up in Blake's bed, naked, a tray on her lap, feeling her heart fill with ashes. With one hand she tugged at the sheet, pulling it up from under the tray on her lap and covering her breasts.

For one night reality had been suspended. One night out of time. One night of magic. It was not enough to change the truth.

Blake didn't really need her, he never had. He could do without her. She was just convenient. And once this was over they would go their separate ways and probably never meet again. Right now, she was just convenient, as she had been convenient when they'd been married.

No, she thought desperately, not again. Not ever again. Her throat closed. Her hands shook and she clamped them around the edge of the tray. She wished she were alone, to deal with her thoughts, to harness the sudden panic rising in her. She wished he would leave.

"Nicky? What's wrong?"

She swallowed convulsively. "I'm not hungry."

"Just like that?"

She nodded, afraid to look at him, afraid to see his face, to see the memories of love in his eyes. I can't let this happen to me, she thought desperately. I can't go through it all again.

She lifted the tray. "Just put it on the table, I'll eat it later." Her voice sounded thin and unreal, as if it didn't belong to her at all. He didn't take the tray from her and she let it rest on her lap again. "I'm not ready to get up yet," she added, hoping that he would go and leave her alone.

"I want to know what's wrong," he said softly.

She shook her head numbly.

"I'm not leaving until you tell me, Nicky."

She knew him well enough to know it made no sense to object or refuse, but she couldn't help herself. "You have no right to demand I tell you anything," she said, but it did not sound convincing.

"I have the right to know why suddenly, after a night like last night, you act as if some disaster has befallen you. Was it something I said? Or did?"

No, it wasn't. Everything had been right and perfect and wonderful beyond words.

A fantasy not rooted in reality.

She stared blindly at the tray on her lap. "It was a mistake. It was my fault. I shouldn't have cooked that dinner, it—"

"What are you talking about?"

"Last night." She took in a shuddering breath. "It was too much like...like before."

"Like when we were married," he said quietly.

She nodded.

"And what was wrong with that?"

"Because it wasn't real last night! It was just...like acting out an old story."

"I rather liked the old story," he said evenly. "But I don't believe either one of us was acting last night. It was very real to me." He took her hand. "Nicky, look at me. Tell me, what went wrong with the old story?"

She gulped in air. "You didn't need me. I mean, not really."

There was a silence. "I don't know what you're talking about, Nicky," he said softly.

"Just what I said. It was always...good when you came home and I was there to make things special. But when I wasn't there, it didn't matter to you. I was convenient, but not essential.'' Bitterness spilled over in her voice. She could taste it in her mouth. ''You didn't need me at all. You did just fine without me.'' She looked down at the tray, silent. The coffee was getting cold. The French toast was getting cold. The air shivered with tension.

''I did just fine without you?'' he repeated slowly. ''How could you possibly know how I was doing when you weren't around?''

She felt an upsurge of uncontrollable emotion. She lifted her gaze to meet his. ''You were never even home when I called you! Not even at three in the night!'' She jerked upright, knocking over the coffee. The tray slid off the bed, crashed onto the floor. Food went flying everywhere. She was beyond caring, beyond reason. All she was feeling was the old anguish searing her soul. Her whole body trembled with it. ''Where were you at night? Where did you sleep and with whom?''

CHAPTER TEN

NICKY had never found an answer to that question. She'd never asked him. She remembered lying in bed in Sophie's spacious apartment in Rome, calculating the time it was in Washington. Four o'clock in the night in Rome, ten in the evening at home. Blake should be home.

She hadn't seen Blake in months and she couldn't stand it anymore. She was going to tell him she was coming home, that she missed him too much. She loved him. She wanted to be with him.

If only he loved her, too. If only he missed her and wanted to be with her.

She slipped out of bed and tiptoed into the living room so as not to wake Sophie, who slept so lightly these days, afraid she wouldn't hear the baby. Using her phone card so her own number would be charged, Nicky dialed and waited.

The phone rang. Once, twice. The answering machine picked up on the fourth ring. Saying nothing, Nicky put the receiver down, her chest tight. Blake wasn't there. Maybe he was in the shower and hadn't heard the phone ringing. Maybe he was having dinner at the house of friends and not yet home. She'd wait half an hour and try again.

She watched the minutes go by on the clock, trying to read a magazine, not even seeing it was in Italian, which she couldn't read, until several minutes later. After twenty minutes she couldn't stand it anymore and dialed again.

No one picked up.

Don't be stupid, she told herself. Go to bed. Go to sleep.

She flitted in and out of slumber, stirring back into wakefulness when she heard the baby crying. She lay still, listening to the movement of feet, the sound of hushed voices. The baby stopped crying.

It was almost six. That made it almost midnight at home. He'd be sleeping. She'd wake him. I don't care, she thought, and slipped on her robe. Quietly she moved back to the living room and picked up the phone once again, her hands shaking as she punched in the numbers. Again the click of the answering machine at the fourth ring. She put the receiver down and hugged herself. Huddling in the corner of the sofa, she tried not to panic. What if he'd been in an accident? What if he was in the hospital? In pain? Dying?

It was all her fault. She should have been home, where she belonged.

She made herself wait to call Blake again until after she'd dressed and had breakfast. It was now one-thirty in the night in Washington, and again the phone rang and rang. There was a telephone right next to Blake's side of the bed; there was no way he could not hear it, no matter how deeply he slept.

She put the receiver down and took in an unsteady breath, clasping her hands tightly together in her lap. Sophie, still in her robe, came into the room on her bare feet and sat down next to her.

She gave a wan smile. She looked tired. "He's not there?" she asked unnecessarily.

"No," Nicky said dully.

At noon, when it was six in the morning in Washington, she called again. No answer. Later again, she called the World Bank, where a snotty secretary informed her Blake was in a meeting and could not be disturbed.

Her heart turned over. Blake was at work. He was not dead or in the hospital. A wave of relief washed over her, followed by new apprehension. Where had he been all night?

"Just tell him his wife called from Rome," she told the secretary and hung up.

She was beginning to feel like a neurotic wife, suspicious and angry.

She *was* suspicious and angry.

Three hours later, Blake called her.

"Nicky? I had a message you called."

"Yes." She swallowed. *I'm coming home*, she wanted to say, but something kept her from saying the words. *I miss you.* How often had she said those words? Countless times, when she called him while he was in hotel rooms far away, gone for weeks on his business trips. *I love you, I miss you. I can't wait for you to be home again.* Such delicious anticipation, always— counting the days, dreaming, fantasizing.

But now she swallowed the words and a painful yearning lodged in her throat. It was his turn to say the words. It was his turn to tell her how he felt, that he wanted her, that he loved her, that he dreamed of her at night. She squeezed her eyes tightly, willing him, from across miles of ocean, to say the words.

"Nicky?" came his voice. "Everything all right? Are Sophie and the baby doing okay?"

"Yes, yes, everything is fine." Disappointment tasted bitter in her mouth and she struggled for control. "What about you? How are you doing?"

"I'm having my usual struggles with the bureaucracy. If ever I take a desk job, tie me up and call a psychiatrist."

In spite of everything she found herself smiling. "I'll do that."

"I've got to go. We have another crisis on our hands and I have to calm some distressed souls. Did you call for any particular reason?" His voice was more businesslike now, his mind set on going back to work already.

Her throat closed. *Yes*, she answered silently. *Your wife's in crisis, too. What about her distressed soul?* Tears burned behind her eyes. "No," she said into the phone. "No particular reason." *Please tell me you love me. Please tell me you miss me.*

"Say hello to Sophie for me," he said. "And I'll see you...next month, after I get back from Guatemala."

She closed her eyes, seeing in her mind his face, the calm eyes, the strong chin. He'd be wearing a business suit, a tie, looking tall and dynamic, emanating confidence. She knew the way the women would look at him in the office and she felt a hot stab of jealousy. She fought against it, her body rigid.

"Yes. 'Bye, Blake."

Sophie came back into the room. "He called you," she stated.

"Yes."

"Everything all right?"

"He's not dead or in the hospital," Nicky said with a grimace of self-derision.

"That's a very good thing." Sophie's tone was dry. "Did he tell you where he was last night?"

Nicky shook her head. "No."

"Didn't you ask?"

"No."

Sophie bit her lip and studied her for a long moment. "You know," she said slowly, "there could be all kinds of explanations."

"I know." She forced a smile. "I'm probably just overreacting."

Three days later she found it hard to still believe she was overreacting. During business hours Blake was at the office, although she would hang up the phone or make an excuse before he'd come on the line. She'd called their home number at all hours of the night three nights in a row. He was never there.

Nicky sat amid the ravages of her breakfast and fought the tears as she remembered the agonizing nights spent dialing her home phone number. Furious, humiliating tears. She looked at Blake, seeing nothing but a blur. "You weren't in our bed, so whose bed were you sleeping in?" Her voice was thick with tears. Her throat ached.

His jaw tensed into steel. There was an icy silence. "Perhaps," he said slowly, ominously, "I'm the one who should ask *you* the same thing! Who were you sleepng with when you didn't come home to be with me?"

She thought her heart would stop. Anger and anguish flooded her. She wiped at her tears. "How dare you!" she whispered fiercely. "I didn't sleep with anybody! How *dare* you think I cheated on you!"

"Considering the circumstances, sweetheart, it was really easy." His mouth twisted bitterly. "Obviously, you were not at all interested in sleeping with me anymore, or you would have managed to come home."

The next thing she saw was his back, then the door slammed closed behind him. She stared at the destruction on the bed—coffee soaking into the sheets and blanket, papaw splattered on the floor, honey dripping from the upturned tray. A picture of her life, her love— everything sweet and lovely, wasted, spoiled.

She was trembling uncontrollably. She curled up into a ball and sobbed.

It took her a long time to put herself back together again, to clean up the mess, to put clean sheets on the bed.

Ramyah had enough to do; she could at least clean up the destruction she had caused herself.

She went back to her own room and tried to write. She felt sick, then remembered she hadn't had breakfast. In the kitchen she found something to eat. Blake was on the veranda, reading a computer printout, writing in the margins. Her eyes filled with tears again. Oh, God, she couldn't stand being here alone with him. She loved him, but it wasn't enough.

He came suddenly to his feet, and a moment later he was in the kitchen. The dark flash in his eyes gave away that he had not expected to see her there. Without a word he reached for the coffeepot and poured himself a cup. He picked up the mug, then set it down again. He put both hands on the counter, as if for support, as if his shoulders carried an enormous burden. He lowered his head and stared straight down at the countertop.

"For what's it's worth," he said tightly, the words coming with difficulty, "I was never, *never* unfaithful to you."

Her mouth went dry. He straightened his back, picked up the coffee cup and left the kitchen without looking at her again.

The dinner party at Ghita's house was that evening. Nicky wore the long *batek* dress again; it was the best she could do under the circumstances. The few things Blake had brought back from her father's house were just simple day clothes, and anything Lisette might have would be too big.

Ghita wore a wine-colored silk dress that could have come straight from a Rome or Paris boutique, and next to her Nicky felt quite the tourist in her *batek* print dress. Ghita's mother was resplendent in a gorgeous, shimmering silk sari. She was a charming woman and made Nicky feel comfortable and welcome, and before long

Nicky was talking to her about Indian curries and chutneys and all manner of Indian kitchen lore.

There were several other guests present and it was a relief to be among people again. The conversation was interesting, the food wonderful, and she was grateful for the diversion.

She tried not to notice how Ghita was keeping Blake entertained, and how he certainly seemed comfortable with her attentions. He was laughing. It made him look less hard, smoothing the sharp edges of his face and lightening the tarnished look in his eyes. Nicky felt a painful twist in her chest. She'd hardly seen him laugh in the days they had been together.

She could not deny a sense of irritation every time her gaze caught the two of them. Irritation ... was that what it was? Ghita was in love with him, she knew that, and the knowledge gave her a queasy feeling in her stomach, in spite of her rational thoughts about the subject: If Blake loved Ghita, he'd have made his moves a long time ago.

Over the years she'd thought of Blake, wondering where he was, and with whom, visualizing him with another woman. But the image was always so excruciatingly painful that she'd push it out of her consciousness immediately. Now, in front of her very eyes, was a real-life woman wanting him, fawning over him, and it made her feel sick with misery.

She needed some air and she slipped away into the garden. The air was fragrant with jasmine and the sky was studded with stars and a silvery crescent moon.

A perfect setting for romance. Her chest hurt as if someone was squeezing the life out of her. Despair settled like wet cement in her stomach. She loved Blake and it was useless. She loved him and it was not enough.

Slowly, she made her way back to the veranda, where an eccentric British professor claimed her attention with a bizarre tale from Colonial times, until Blake told her it was time to leave.

Earlier, the drive to the Patels' house had been tense and silent, as had been the lunch they'd shared that afternoon. The trip back home was not much different. They said little apart from some casual comments and Nicky was glad when they finally reached the house.

She wished Blake good night, went into her room and crawled into bed. She felt exhausted, as if she'd done heavy physical labor all day.

In spite of her fatigue, she couldn't sleep. Her mind was in turmoil, her thoughts running around in chaos. She tried to still her mind, thinking of peaceful scenes, but it was useless. An hour later she got up in frustration, put on Lisette's robe and went to the kitchen to make some tea.

She took it to the veranda, smelling the burning mosquito coils as soon as she stepped outside. Blake was sitting in the darkness, a glass in his hand.

"Couldn't sleep?" he asked.

"No. I made some tea."

He waved at a chair. "Have a seat."

She swallowed. "No, no. I don't want to disturb you if you want to be alone."

"I've been alone enough." His voice was level, yet with a faint hint of something else—some other, deeper meaning.

I've been alone enough, too, she thought miserably.

"Sit down, Nicky," he said quietly.

She sat down, knowing that Blake's presence most likely was not going to calm her frayed nerves. Drinking her tea, she stared out into the darkness, listening to the shrill, frantic buzzing of cicadas in the forest. The sound grated on her nerves.

"You mentioned a dream Friday night at dinner," Blake said a moment later. "I wonder if you'd tell me about it."

She frowned. "Why?"

He shrugged. "I thought about what you said, and it struck me as...odd for you to have a dream about being rescued."

"Odd? Why?" She put the teacup on the table.

"It seems out of character. You're not the type waiting around to be rescued. You've always been so independent and self-reliant."

True enough, she had to admit. She stared at the smoke of the mosquito coils spiraling lazily into the air.

Blake shifted in his chair, the rattan creaking under his weight. "So, tell me, why did you dream about being rescued? An independent person like you?"

"I don't know."

"Will you tell me about it?"

She felt gripped by a strange mood. It was a night filled with shadows—shadows and secrets and sorrows.

"I dreamed that I was alone in a big, empty house," she began. "I never knew whose it was, but it was in a strange, cold place, far away. It was standing by itself in a big, open space and I could see the horizon all around. I was looking out the window and I was waiting for you, but I didn't think you'd find me because you didn't know where I was."

"I always knew where you were," he said softly.

"I know." She swallowed. "But this was a dream. And in the dream I had forgotten to tell you. And I was so afraid you wouldn't find me because it was such a strange place and I didn't know where it was or how I had gotten there. It was so barren and empty and there were no trees. Can you imagine a place without trees?" She bit her lip, knowing nervous energy made her keep talking, as if now that she had started, she wouldn't know how to stop.

"Anyway, I'd been waiting for you for a long time, but I don't know how long, and then finally I saw you riding up on a horse."

"A horse? I haven't been on a horse since I was a kid at summer camp."

"Dreams are weird sometimes."

"Then what happened?"

She looked away, aware of the nervous beating of her heart. "You . . . I went outside and you just lifted me up with one arm and put me in front of you on the horse and off we went."

He gave a half smile. "Just like that?"

"No, yes. Sort of."

"What else, then?" His voice was low, the smile gone.

She hesitated. "Nothing, I mean, I don't really remember."

This was a lie, of course. But there was no way she could reveal to him now what he'd said to her in the dream, or what had happened after. She came to her feet and moved to the veranda railing and rested her arms on top of it.

She heard his chair creak as he stood up and then he was behind her, turning her around to face her. She had her back against the railing, and he was leaning close, his hand resting on the railing on either side of her, caging her in.

She stiffened instinctively. "Don't do this to me."

"Do what?"

"Make me feel trapped!"

His mouth curved in faint amusement. "But you are," he said meaningfully.

"Do you think this is funny?"

"No, actually it's not." His hands fell away from the railing, but he did not step away from her.

She sighed. "What do you want?" She could smell the clean, familiar scent of him, felt her body begin to tremble with the awareness of his closeness. She fought against it, knowing it was futile.

"I want you to tell me what I said to you when I put you on my horse."

"It was just a stupid dream!" she said tightly.

"Maybe not so stupid."

"Oh, for God's sake!" she said irritably. "All right, I'll tell you. And then I want to go inside. I want to go to sleep."

"Fine."

She braced her feet against the wooden boards of the veranda, willing herself to be calm. "You told me you were taking me home because that's where I belonged," she said in a flat monotone. "And that you would find me wherever I went because you loved me and wanted me with you."

A short silence. "And then," Blake said, "you yelled at me saying you were a free person and I had no right to make you do anything or force you to go anywhere, not even home if that's not where you wanted to be."

She stared at his chin, her throat suddenly dry. She was too afraid to meet his eyes. "No, I didn't."

"Why not?"

She closed her eyes for a moment. "I was so relieved you had come for me."

I was so relieved that you wanted me enough to come and get me.

He frowned. "Were you in danger? What was I rescuing you from?"

She shook her head. "There wasn't any danger, not anything physical, anyway. I was alone."

"I see. Then what happened?" he asked. "We drove off into the sunset together?"

She swallowed. "No."

"Then what?"

"We rode only for a short distance and then you suddenly stopped the horse and put me back on the ground again."

"Where were we then?"

She shook her head. "Nowhere. There was nothing anywhere, just emptiness. And you told me that, after all, you could not rescue me." She bit her lip, hard. "You said I had to rescue myself. And then you rode off and left me." Her voice cracked. "I started screaming for you and every time I had the dream, that's when I'd wake up. Always like that."

She shivered in the silence. Finally she glanced up, seeing him gazing down at her, his face pale in the moonlight. But it was his eyes that shocked her most—dull gray and full of desolation.

The expression was gone in a flash. His jaw hardened. "Well," he said flatly. "I was a real hero, wasn't I?"

"It was only a dream."

He searched her face in the dark. "Right." He turned abruptly and picked up his glass from the table. "Better drink your tea," he said evenly, "before it gets cold."

Nicky knocked on the office door, not wanting to disturb Blake, but having no choice. She sucked at her finger, where a tiny thorn had lodged itself under her skin. After lunch she'd been restless and gone out to pick a bunch of flowers to cheer up her room and had found herself attacked by something thorny.

"Come in." The staccato sound of typing did not stop.

She opened the door. "Sorry to bother you, but I need tweezers and I can't find any. Do you have some I could borrow?" She'd searched through the bathroom medicine cabinet and come up with nothing.

He ganced up, absently. "Tweezers? Yes. In the top drawer of the dresser in my room. They're in a little white first-aid box."

"Thanks."

She went in his room and opened the dresser drawer, scanning the contents. Plane tickets, his wallet, a bunch of keys, a stack of expense receipts held together with a big red paper clip. A passport. Another passport.

She picked both of them up, her heart racing with trepidation as she opened the covers.

One was his. The other was hers.

CHAPTER ELEVEN

NICKY stared at her own picture, her body flooding with
fury. He had taken her passport and told her it had been
stolen. Or at least had made her think it had. *Obviously,
someone took it*, he'd told her. Well, obviously someone
had. He, himself.

As long as he had her passport, she'd be unable to
leave the country. He was keeping her here against her
will because her father wanted her here. Her father
wanted to protect his little girl and Blake was his loyal
ally.

Movement behind her. She swung around, seeing
Blake come into the bedroom, a wry look on his face.

"I see you found it," he commented. "I was mo-
mentarily caught off guard." His tone was dry. "I'm
not in the habit of harboring secrets."

"I don't believe you did this!" Her voice was low with
rage. "You knew I wanted to leave!"

He pushed his hands into his shorts' pockets and observed her calmly. "But I didn't want you to go."

"Why?" she snapped. "So you'd have some easy sex
handy?" She gave a mocking laugh. "Surely you could
have found it a lot easier somewhere else."

A look of distaste crossed his features. "Don't be
crude. It's not your style."

His high-handedness fueled her rage. "What do you
know about my style? You haven't seen me for years!
Why did you force me to stay here with you? Because
of my father? His wishes are more important than

mine?'' She anchored her feet to the floor to keep her knees from shaking.

"Your father's wishes were not my main concern."

"Oh, and what was?"

"My own. I thought it was high time we spent some time together."

"So you kept me here against my will?" She could not believe this. He had never before forced her to do anything. It was against everything he'd always believed in—that it was important to leave each other free to make personal decisions, not to interfere with each other's professional life.

"I'm sorry it was against your will," he said calmly. "I thought you might enjoy being here."

"I don't enjoy being forced to do anything! Why did you steal my passport?"

His mouth quirked. "You do have a flair for the dramatic, don't you? I didn't steal it. I took it initially fully intending to give it to you," he said. "You asked me to get it for you."

"But you didn't give it to me!" she said hotly.

"I changed my mind."

"Why? Why didn't you help me leave the country and be done with this little rescue mission of yours?"

"I wanted you with me." A stormy tension hovered deep in his eyes. "I always wanted you with me. I don't like empty houses and empty hotel rooms."

"Oh, really?" she snapped. "For not liking that, you sure love those trips all over the world!" She tossed Blake's passport back into the drawer and shoved it close. She put her own in her shorts' pocket.

"Traveling is part of the job." He paused, his eyes turning darker. "You know what I used to like most about traveling when we were still married?" he asked then, his voice low.

"Being alone?"

He shook his head. "No."

"Well, you could have fooled me!" she said bitterly.

He looked at her bleakly. "What I liked most, Nicky, was coming home to you."

Her heart lurched painfully. She stared at him, the anger ebbing away.

His eyes were a misty gray as he held her gaze. "I loved coming home and finding you cooking up a storm," he said softly, "the house full of lilacs or roses or whatever smelled nice. I loved taking you in my arms and knowing you were all mine, that you had been waiting for me and made everything special and beautiful for me—because you loved me, because you were happy to have me home again. I felt so... rich."

A grieving pain swirled through her, filling the bitter spaces, giving no better comfort. Hot tears stung her eyes. "I didn't know you felt that way," she said tremulously. "Why didn't you ever tell me?"

He stared at her, a stunned expression in his eyes. "Nicky, surely you *knew*?"

She swallowed. "I thought I did. In the beginning it was so good, and then..." She stopped, took in a shaky breath and sat down on the edge of the bed.

"Then what?"

She covered her face with her hands. "I started to think you were just taking me for granted. That time I went to visit my parents in Morocco and I wasn't home when you came home... we talked on the phone and something happened. I don't know."

He took a few steps toward her, stood in front of her. "*What* happened, Nicky?" His voice was urgent. "I don't understand. I never understood."

She gulped in air. "I thought you didn't care whether I would be home or not. You said nothing about missing me. You said nothing about wanting me to be home."

"Your mother was sick. You needed to be with her. How could I possibly worry about what I wanted for myself? Besides, we had an agreement, we made a promise to let each other be free."

She closed her eyes. "I wanted to know that you needed me. I never felt you needed me."

"Nicky, how could you not *know*?"

"You never told me!"

His eyes flared with amazement. "I didn't tell you? No, maybe not in words, but surely I showed you?"

She clenched her hands in her lap. "I don't know! I needed to *hear* it. I needed you to *tell* me! You never told me anything! You never told me what you thought or how you felt!"

He didn't move. He stared at her like a statue. "My, God, Nicky," he said unsteadily. "I—"

Noises interrupted his words. Ramyah stood in the open bedroom door, her eyes huge, trembling, rattling off a stream of Malay.

Blake was gone in an instant, Ramyah rushing after him. Nicky followed them on instinct. She had no idea what Ramyah had said and what was going on, but it was clearly serious. She found them outside, bending over Ali, the gardener, whose leg was bleeding profusely from a gaping wound. His gardening machete lay next to him in the grass.

Nicky felt the blood drain from her face at the sight of it. She took in a steadying breath. What they really didn't need now was for her to faint to the ground. She forced air into her lungs.

"What can I do?" she asked.

"Get some towels and something to make a bandage with." Blake's voice was short and clipped.

She raced inside, found what he'd asked for and brought it back outside. "Did he cut an artery?"

"No, thank God, but it's not pretty. He'll need some serious stitching up." Blake tended to the moaning Ali quickly and efficiently.

"How did this happen?" Nicky asked.

"He tripped and fell with the machete in his hand. Help me get him into the car, will you?"

They settled Ali onto the back seat of the Land Cruiser to take him to the nearest hospital. Ramyah sat down in the front next to Blake, who motioned for Nicky to get in, too.

"I don't want you staying here all by yourself without even a phone," he said.

She couldn't find a rational argument against it, certainly not while being confronted with what could happen accidentally, in a flash of time. So she squeezed in next to Ramyah and they took off down the rutted track.

They drove to the Patels' house where Blake used the phone and told Nicky to stay right there until he came back for her later that day. Mrs. Patel smiled at her, saying it was no problem at all.

She felt like a child being left with a baby-sitter, but she had little choice. Getting Ali to the hospital was the main issue. She became aware of the small thorn still in her hand, the spot feeling hot to the touch. Well, it would keep until they got back home later today. She'd forgotten about it in the midst of all the commotion.

Ghita was out playing tennis, Mrs. Patel told her, and was expected back anytime. She appeared twenty minutes later, looking gorgeous in tennis whites, and the three of them had afternoon tea. After which Mrs. Patel disappeared into the kitchen and Nicky was left to the mercies of Ghita, who was cool but polite. Nicky decided to pretend not to notice and kept up a cheery conversation, which was a bit one-sided. Until at one point Ghita took a deep breath, looked straight at her and apparently was gearing up to make an announcement. Nicky watched her, wondering what was coming.

"There's something I think you should know," Ghita began. "I...I know you're in love with Blake."

Nicky felt a jolt of surprise at the rather blunt comment. "You do?" she asked, putting a good dose of derision in her voice.

"Yes. I know you told me it's just a temporary...situation, but I'm not blind. When you were here for dinner Saturday night it was very obvious how you feel about him."

Nicky felt anger creep through her. "The nature of my relationship with Blake is none of your business and I have no intention of discussing it with you." Who did Ghita think she was, for heaven's sake?

"Perhaps not, but let me just tell you that if you harbor any hopes for permanency with Blake, you'd do yourself a big favor by abandoning them."

"I remember you telling me that before, yes. And why is that?"

"Because he's not getting married again."

"And how do you know that?"

Ghita laughed dryly. "Believe me, I know. He won't even marry me, and I've loved him for years and years." She looked away, and Nicky saw a glimmer of tears in her eyes. "I can't believe this," Ghita went on in a tight, low voice. "I can't believe what this woman did to him!"

Nicky stiffened. This woman. His wife. Her.

"What did she do to him?" What possessed her to ask the question?

Anger leapt into Ghita's dark eyes. "She destroyed him! He was here, shortly after she told him she wanted a divorce, and I hardly recognized him. I thought he had died but was still walking. I...I..." Her voice trailed away and she looked helplessly down at her hands clasped in her lap.

"Excuse me," said Nicky, and came to her feet. She almost ran back into the house, only to practically collide with the subject of their discussion. Her heart leapt in her throat. She wanted to cry. She wanted to die. She wanted to wake up out of this nightmare from the past.

He steadied her with a hand on her shoulder, looking at her with narrowed eyes. "What's wrong?"

She was trembling. She gulped in air. "Nothing," she said thickly, praying for composure. She took in another deep breath. "You're back," she stated unnecessarily. "How's Ali?"

He studied her face, frowning. "He'll be all right, but they wanted to keep him for observation."

Mrs. Patel, who'd escorted him into the sitting room, offered drinks and invited them to stay for dinner, which Blake declined, saying he was dirty and tired and not fit for company.

A short time later they were back in the car on the way back home. The sun was setting, bathing the scenery in a pale golden glow. The world seemed calm and peaceful, which was not a feeling Nicky was experiencing sitting next to the quiet Blake.

"Where's Ramyah?" she asked.

"She's with Ali. She'll stay the night at the house of relatives in Ipoh." A few more details followed. Then silence reigned again. It was not a comfortable silence. The confrontation in Blake's bedroom earlier that afternoon was still alive between them.

Unfinished business, she thought. He's going to want to talk some more. She pressed her eyes shut and leaned back in the car seat, her chest heavy with apprehension.

It was completely dark when they arrived at the house. Inside Blake turned on the living room lights and asked if she wanted a drink.

"I'll wait," she said, rubbing her bare arms. "I want to have a shower first, and put on something warmer."

The evening chill had set in and she felt cold in her thin cotton dress.

The shower felt good, and she tried to let the warm water sooth the tension out of her, but wasn't successful. Her frazzled nerves were beyond soothing. She wished she could just go to bed and avoid seeing Blake for the rest of the evening. But it was still early and they hadn't had anything to eat yet. She pulled on one of Lisette's roomy sweat suits against the cool night and went back to the living room. Blake was sitting in a chair, a glass of whiskey in his hand. He was not reading or doing anything, just sitting there with the almost-empty glass in his hand.

He glanced at her as she came into the room. "Did you ever get that thorn out of your hand?" he asked.

"Actually, no. It's still in there."

"Let me see."

She showed him her hand. "It's nothing."

He held her hand and examined it. "I'll get the tweezers. It doesn't look happy."

It was not worth arguing over, so she said nothing while he tried to extract the little splinter, which was being terribly stubborn. He was very close and she studied his face as he concentrated on her hand—the planes and angles, the lines fanning out at the corners of his eyes, the beginning of a beard stubble. She loved that face.

I thought he had died but was still walking. Ghita's voice came back to her. She bit her lip and tears sprang up in her eyes. Oh, God, she thought, what did I do to him?

Blake glanced up at her. "Am I hurting you?"

"Yes, no." She bit her lip. "Don't worry about it. Just get it out." Please just get it out. She felt like she was going to shatter into a million pieces. Not because of the thorn, although it didn't feel exactly wonderful to have him digging into her hand.

He was so close. She could reach out and put her hands on his hair. If she leaned a little closer she could touch his face with her own.

He straightened away from her. "Got it. Stubborn little sucker."

"Thank you." Her voice sounded thick.

"I'm sorry I hurt you."

She shook her head. "It's nothing." She came to her feet. "I'll find us something to eat." There was a hollow feeling inside her—painful. Maybe it was just hunger. Maybe not.

He tossed back the last of his drink. "You want some help?"

She shook her head. "I'll do something simple. Are you very hungry?"

"No. Something simple will be fine."

So polite. So calm on the surface. Underneath the words she felt a storm of emotions brewing. She was relieved to be alone in the kitchen and she took her time washing lettuce and cutting up cold chicken and cheese and slicing mushrooms and onions and tomatoes.

She was just about finished when he came into the kitchen, bringing with him a fresh scent of soap. His hair was damp and he wore a clean pair of jeans and a pale gray sweatshirt. He looked so good. She closed her eyes. Why did he have to look so—so overwhelmingly...male?

He poured them a glass of wine and they ate the salad, but she hardly tasted anything and she had trouble swallowing. She drank the wine and had another glass.

When they were finished eating, he came to his feet, cleared the table and rinsed the dishes, leaving them in the sink.

"I think we have a conversation to finish," he stated, turning to face her.

Her heart leapt in her throat. She'd known it was coming, yet she didn't feel prepared. She never would be. She followed him into the sitting room.

She sat down on the sofa and he lowered himself next to her. "We never did much talking about what went on in our marriage, did we?" he asked.

"No. We weren't home enough, I suppose."

"But when we were home, we didn't, either. I was never aware we had any problems when we were home together." He paused. "When we were home together, we were happy. That's all I ever remember. Being happy."

Her throat closed and she couldn't say a word. It was true. Whenever they'd been together, she'd been happy.

"I want to know," he went on, the words coming out with difficulty, "whenever we were home together, were you ever unhappy? Was there something I didn't see?"

She shook her head, and still her throat would make no sound.

"When then did things go wrong? When did you start being unhappy?"

She swallowed at the constriction in her voice. "When we weren't together anymore."

He stared at her. "And a divorce was a solution for that?"

"No." She closed her eyes briefly. "I thought you didn't care that we never saw each other anymore. I asked for a divorce to shake you up, to wake you up." She gulped in air, feeling overwhelmed by the memories—the old pain and anger. "And you didn't even fight it!" she went on, her voice rising. "I wanted you to refuse, to fight it. I..." She could not go on. She felt a sob struggle in her throat as she looked at him.

She saw the color leave his face. "Nicky," he said hoarsely, "what are you saying? Are you telling me you didn't *want* a divorce?"

CHAPTER TWELVE

THE moment of truth. Blake's question hovered between them, alive and quivering.

"Yes! No! I mean—" Her lungs dragged in air. "No, I didn't want a divorce." The admission struggled painfully out of her.

"Why in God's name did you tell me you wanted one?"

"I wanted to shake you up!" Desperation in her voice.

"*Shake me up*?" His voice was low with shock. "Oh, Nicky, I was plenty shaken up!"

Her whole body went rigid. "I didn't know! You didn't tell me! I wanted you to tell me what you felt, what you wanted! I wanted you to *care*!"

"Oh, my God," he whispered. "Oh, my God, Nicky, this is insane! What made you think I didn't care?"

Her mouth felt dry. She swallowed with difficulty. "For one thing, you signed the papers. You didn't even come home. If you cared, why didn't you fight the divorce?"

He gave a harsh little laugh. "I wasn't going to keep you against your will! If you didn't want to be with me, if you wanted out, what choice did I have but let you go?"

"*Just like that*?"

He shoved his hands into his pockets and his face worked. "No, not just like that, Nicky. You hadn't been home with me for God knows how long. Do you think I want a woman who doesn't want me?"

I did want you! she cried out silently, but the words stayed frozen in her mind. The terrible truth was slowly sinking in. Her own fear and insecurity had made her play a dangerous game in the hope Blake would do what she wanted him to do. She'd tried to force a response from him. She'd been testing him.

Testing him.

Was that what she'd been doing?

Of course that's what she'd been doing. Testing him to see what he would do if she wasn't there for him, to see if he really wanted her. If he would call and tell her to come home...

But he had not known the rules; he had not known what was in her mind and thoughts. And eventually the game had taken on a life of its own and swept her along on a tidal wave of emotion.

And in the end it had been fatal.

The silence was suffocating her. She struggled for air. "You thought I didn't want you?" she whispered finally. It had never occurred to her that he might think that, that he would not know how much she loved him. She'd told him countless times, written it in cards and notes, said it over the phone. Until pain and anger had taken over and she had stopped.

A muscle jerked in his cheek. "What else was I supposed to think, Nicky? You were clearly avoiding being home when I was. Always, there was another reason, another excuse for you to be away. The first couple of times it was because of your mother. I understood that, of course. Then it was Sophie." He shrugged. "I had more trouble with that, knowing that she has a slew of relatives to give her aid and comfort. But I had no intention to interfere, if this is what you wanted." His jaw hardened. "After that...it was that special two-week cooking course in New York you so very suddenly had to attend for the exact two weeks that I would be home after my trip to Guatemala." His eyes were dark with stormy emotion.

She said nothing, feeling a heavy weight of shame and regret. Such a terrible, destructive game she had played—only she hadn't seen it then. She remembered making bargains with God as she was getting ready to go to New York. Please, let him tell me he misses me and can't wait to see me again. If he says anything of the kind, I won't go. I'll stay right here and make everything special for us, like it used to be.

When he had called she'd been out, and the message on the answering machine had been short and businesslike, giving her his flight number and saying he'd take a taxi home from the airport if she'd be unable to pick him up. There'd been nothing about looking forward to seeing her, nothing about having missed her. And that after months of separation.

He doesn't care, she'd thought, and she'd felt something freeze inside her. She'd gone into the bedroom and packed her suitcase to go to New York. How could she be with him at home when she didn't think he loved her anymore?

Blake rubbed his forehead. "Nicky, why did you do that? Why did you go to New York? And don't tell me that course was a once-in-a-lifetime opportunity."

Her heart cringed. The course had been real enough, but it hadn't been important. In New York she'd managed to be even more miserable than she'd been in Rome. She'd hoped Blake would have come to see her for the weekend, if not to ask her to come home. He had not. Again she had called him at all hours of the night, and again he had not been home.

"I was upset...angry," she managed at last.

He stared at her, eyes dark and compelling. "Why? Good Lord, Nicky, what had I done?"

Her throat ached with the effort not to cry. "I didn't think you loved me anymore. You kept telling me how you could manage. You were so...independent and self-reliant and...I didn't feel you needed me."

His face twisted in a wry grimace. "Nicky, I *can* manage. If we're talking about basic human survival needs. I don't need someone to wash my socks and make my bed. I don't need someone to do my cooking. I don't need a housekeeper or a fussing mother. I didn't marry you to fulfill those functions. I married you because I needed a wife, a friend, a lover."

She felt the damp drip of a tear on her hand and she glanced down, seeing nothing but a blur. "You never told me you needed me. All I wanted was for you to tell me you missed me when we were apart." Her voice broke. "I wanted you to tell me you wanted me home when I wasn't."

He came to his feet, raking both hands through his hair—a frustrated, helpless gesture. "I can't believe this," he said on a note of despair. "I was expressing my love for you by not being selfish about what I wanted for myself. By not interfering with your freedom to be who you wanted to be and what you wanted to do. It wasn't because I didn't care."

She closed her eyes, digesting the words, knowing the truth of them, knowing, too, how little she had understood her own husband, the man whom she had loved for his unpossessiveness, his unselfishness and generosity of spirit.

"I never looked at it like that," she said in a small voice, glancing up at him, seeing desolation edged in his features.

He pushed his hands into his pockets and took a few steps away, turned on his heel and came back to where she was sitting.

"And when you no longer came home when I was home," he went on, "I assumed it was because that's how you wanted it." A muscle jerked at his temple. "I wondered if you'd stopped loving me, if you'd found someone else."

"Oh, God," she muttered miserably. "No, no."

"Nicky," he said softly, "what else was I to think?"

She shook her head numbly. Why had she not told him about her worries? Her fears? Would he not have understood? He was her husband. He had married her and promised to love her always. Why, then, had she doubted him?

It was easy to find excuses: She'd been young and inexperienced. They'd been married much too soon. They hadn't known each other well enough. She had not truly understood that Blake did not express himself with words. He was the strong, silent type—she had loved that about him, yet she hadn't had the maturity to know how to deal with it.

Blake sat down again next to her. Not too close, leaving space. Tears blinded her and she wiped at them.

"I'm so sorry," she said thickly. "I'm so sorry."

Across the space between them he took her hand. "I'm sorry, too," he said softly.

"I should have just come out and told you what I needed, told you about why I was so scared. I made so many mistakes, so many stupid mistakes." Her throat ached with the effort not to cry.

"We both did, Nicky. I've never been one to express my feelings, I know that. I took for granted that you knew how I felt about you." Grief and regret darkened his eyes. "I loved you so deeply, Nicky, it did not occur to me that you needed reassurance, that I needed to…to be more verbal about it."

It hurt to see the pain in his face and she lowered her gaze to his ringless left hand resting on his denim-covered thigh. "You...we...we were so far away, and then you'd call, and I was always so happy to hear your voice and then...and then you wouldn't say anything. You were always so businesslike." She glanced up at him. "I was so insecure."

He smiled ruefully. "The phone never struck me as a very romantic piece of equipment for communication. It's what I use for business and other nonintimate matters."

"I so wanted to hear you say you loved me, that you missed me."

"I always missed you. And you were always on my mind—in the middle of a meeting, in the middle of a field of yams or vanilla beans." He gave a wistful little smile. "When you come to think of it, Nicky, you've been thought of, missed and loved, in practically every corner of the world."

Regret twisted inside her. She couldn't make her voice work and she sank her teeth into her lower lip to stop it from trembling.

Blake sighed wearily. "I'm sorry I'm not a romantic on the telephone, whisper words of love, sensuous, intimate stuff." He gave a helpless little groan. "It's not my style, Nicky, but that doesn't mean that I didn't feel all these things. I thought you knew that."

She shook her head numbly.

"When you weren't home anymore, I should have demanded an explanation," he said in a strangled voice. "I should never have let it go on the way it did."

"Why did you?"

He shook his head. "My pride was hurt. The only reason I could come up with was that you found someone else, and I wasn't—"

"Oh, Blake," she whispered, "no, no."

"Do you remember that dream you told me about? The one with me on a horse, rescuing you?"

"Yes."

He rubbed his neck, his eyes bleak. "Every time I came home alone to the house, that's what I wanted to do. I wanted to get on the next plane to wherever you were and simply pick you up and take you home with me. I wanted to tell you I couldn't live without you, that I wanted you, that I loved you more than anything in the whole world and you belonged with me."

How she had hoped and dreamed that he would come—to Morocco, Rome, New York and tell her just those words. "I wanted you to do that," she admitted. "I was always secretly waiting for you to come."

"I was too damned proud. The idea that you didn't want me was not easy to accept, and I wasn't going to beg for your love."

She closed her eyes briefly, stunned by the notion that he might ever have thought he'd have to beg for her love. It filled her with sadness and regret.

What a terrible thing had happened between them.

She thought of the dream, trying to see the meaning. She swallowed painfully and forced herself to look at Blake. "There was truth in what you said in the dream, you know, about my having to rescue myself. I was wrong to sit and wait for you to come for me. I should have rescued myself."

He searched her face. "How?" he asked softly.

"I should have talked about my fears instead of letting them ferment inside of me. I should have been home with you talking about it instead of staying away and worrying whether it mattered to you that I wasn't there."

He gave a weary little smile. "Oh, it mattered to me, Nicky. What do you think? That house was nothing with you not in it—just another place to sleep, another place to eat. Except worse."

"Worse?"

"Because everything reminded me of you, accentuating the fact that you weren't there. At least in a hotel room everything is anonymous and impersonal." His mouth quirked in self-derision. "I couldn't stand being alone in the house, so I'd stay at a hotel near the World Bank office."

She felt an aching regret. "I called and called at all hours of the night," she said, her voice trembling. "And you were never there. I thought you were with someone else."

His face worked. "God, Nicky, what kind of crazy ideas did you have in your head? How could you ever, ever think I wanted anyone but you?"

Tears ran silently down her cheeks. She was afraid to utter another word.

He moved closer to her, taking both her hands in his own. "Nicky, do you have any idea how much I loved you?"

She shook her head. "If I had known I wouldn't have done what I did." She felt the strength of his hands, drawing courage from it. It was so hard to say what she had to say, what she needed to. "I put you to the test," she confessed. "I stayed away to test you. I wanted you to prove yourself, but it had to be on my terms."

"And I didn't know your rules."

"I can't believe I did this. How could I have done this?" She withdrew her hands from his grasp and covered her face. "I don't know what to do," she said on a low moan.

His arms came around her, locking her against him. "You can forgive yourself," he suggested quietly. "You can forgive me. And then I'll have to do the same thing."

She lowered her hands, feeling her face against his shoulder, wanting to curl up closer against him, feel his warmth sooth the grieving sadness inside her. She sat very still. "I can forgive you," she said shakily. "It's not hard at all. But I don't know about forgiving myself."

He lifted her chin and his face was close, his eyes full of tenderness. "I feel exactly the same way. I'm having trouble forgiving myself for my stupid pride. It's a lot easier forgiving you."

She shook her head. "I don't understand. Why is that? I played such a terrible, immature game. It was unfair and dangerous. How can you forgive me for that?"

His mouth tilted in a solemn little smile. "Because I love you more than words could ever express, Nicky."

She sat motionless as the words seeped into her soul. The pain eased out of her chest as jubilant tears filled her eyes.

"Nicky?" His mouth brushed against hers. "I love you. I always did, I always will. I've never wanted anybody but you."

"I love you, too." A sob broke loose and then she was crying uncontrollably, a torrent of emotion freeing her heart, her mind. He held her tight against him.

"We are a sorry pair," he muttered when her body grew limp against him. "You're the verbal one and you can't talk, and I'm the quiet one and now I have to do all the talking. All right, then, here we go. Did I tell you how much I love you? Do you know how much I need you in my life? I need you more than you'll ever understand, Nicky. Please, please, don't ever doubt it."

She nodded against his chest, too choked up to utter a word.

"Say something," he said in her ear.

"I love you," she whispered, and new tears flooded her eyes. "I never stopped loving you."

He stroked her back. "All right, I'll keep talking. This is what we are going to do. Stop me anytime you don't agree. We're going to get married again and do it right this time around. If I feel unhappy about something, I will tell you. If you feel unhappy or worried about something you will tell me. How is this so far?"

She nodded, burying her wet face against his chest, savoring the comfort, the words.

"All right, then," he went on, "this agreement we used to have about letting each other be free is out the door, gone and finished. You are not free to do just any crazy thing you want to, and neither am I. Rest assured, that if you get yourself into trouble again, I'm not going to stand by and let you. I will come and rescue you— both of us. We belong together, and if one of us is in trouble, then we both are."

She gave a tremulous smile, still saying nothing, listening to the most wonderful voice in the world. He lifted her chin and kissed her. She kissed him back with a euphoric sense of relief and abandon. "I love you," she whispered against his mouth. "I love you, I love you."

With a soft groan, he lifted her up as he came to his feet and carried her into the bedroom.

"Have I told you," he whispered as he began to take off her clothes, "that sometimes all I have to do is just look at you and know that you are all I want? Just you. In the house with me, next to me, in bed with me. Forever."

She felt a flowering of joy, of exultation. "I'll be there," she said tremulously. "I promise you I'll always be there."

ℋarlequin Romance®

celebrates forty fabulous years!

Crack open the champagne and join us in celebrating Harlequin Romance's very special birthday.

Forty years of bringing you the best in romance fiction—and the best just keeps getting better!

Not only are we promising you three months of terrific books, authors and romance, but a chance to win a special hardbound 40th Anniversary collection featuring three of your favorite Harlequin Romance authors. And 150 lucky readers will receive an **autographed** collector's edition. Truly a one-of-a-kind keepsake.

Look in the back pages of any Harlequin Romance title, from April to June for more details.

Come join the party!

Look us up on-line at: http://www.romance.net

HR40THG2

Take 4 bestselling love stories FREE

Plus get a FREE surprise gift!

Special Limited-time Offer

Mail to Harlequin Reader Service®

3010 Walden Avenue
P.O. Box 1867
Buffalo, N.Y. 14240-1867

YES! Please send me 4 free Harlequin Presents® novels and my free surprise gift. Then send me 6 brand-new novels every month, which I will receive months before they appear in bookstores. Bill me at the low price of $2.90 each plus 25¢ delivery and applicable sales tax, if any*. That's the complete price and a savings of over 10% off the cover prices—quite a bargain! I understand that accepting the books and gift places me under no obligation ever to buy any books. I can always return a shipment and cancel at any time. Even if I never buy another book from Harlequin, the 4 free books and the surprise gift are mine to keep forever.

106 BPA A3UL

Name	(PLEASE PRINT)	
Address	Apt. No.	
City	State	Zip

This offer is limited to one order per household and not valid to present Harlequin Presents® subscribers. *Terms and prices are subject to change without notice. Sales tax applicable in N.Y.

UPRES-696   ©1990 Harlequin Enterprises Limited

Free Gift Offer

With a Free Gift proof-of-purchase
from any Harlequin® book, you can receive
a beautiful cubic zirconia pendant.

This stunning marquise-shaped stone is a genuine cubic
zirconia—accented by an 18" gold tone necklace.
(Approximate retail value $19.95)

Send for yours today...
compliments of HARLEQUIN®

To receive your free gift, a cubic zirconia pendant, send us one original proof-of-purchase, photocopies not accepted, from the back of any Harlequin Romance®, Harlequin Presents®, Harlequin Temptation®, Harlequin Superromance®, Harlequin Intrigue®, Harlequin American Romance®, or Harlequin Historicals® title available at your favorite retail outlet, together with the Free Gift Certificate, plus a check or money order for $1.65 U.S./$2.15 CAN. (do not send cash) to cover postage and handling, payable to Harlequin Free Gift Offer. We will send you the specified gift. Allow 6 to 8 weeks for delivery. Offer good until December 31, 1997, or while quantities last. Offer valid in the U.S. and Canada only.

Free Gift Certificate

Name: _____

Address: _____

City: _____ State/Province: _____ Zip/Postal Code: _____

Mail this certificate, one proof-of-purchase and a check or money order for postage and handling to: HARLEQUIN FREE GIFT OFFER 1997. In the U.S.: 3010 Walden Avenue, P.O. Box 9071, Buffalo NY 14269-9057. In Canada: P.O. Box 604, Fort Erie, Ontario L2Z 5X3.